HIS PERFECT COMPANION

ALEXA MILNE

His Perfect Companion
ISBN # 978-1-83943-899-8
©Copyright Alexa Milne 2019
Cover Art by Erin Dameron-Hill ©Copyright June 2020
Interior text design by Claire Siemaszkiewicz
Pride Publishing

HIS PERFECT
COMPANION

Dedication

I'm so happy I got a chance to rewrite this story that gives Mick and Ceri a proper ending. I'd like to thank Cath and Dawn who read the original and read this version along with Jacqui. I'd also like to thank Rebecca for making my words better. Lastly, this is dedicated to the Doctor and all his companions. Without them, I suspect this, and all my other stories, would never have been written.

Chapter One

"Caught you."

Mick jumped and nearly tipped out of his chair. He switched camera screen and hoped his blush wasn't obvious. At least he'd hidden his knitting away in his bag. "Shouldn't you be cleaning somewhere?" he asked Ruby. "Reception, if I'm not mistaken."

She didn't move. "I don't blame you looking. He is rather striking with his hair changing color every week."

Mick glared at her and tapped his badge. "It's my job to monitor everyone in the building."

"Yeah, yeah, but some people are worth watching more than others." She flicked a duster in his direction and gave him one of those smiles that suggested she knew something he didn't.

"You'll be late if you don't get going now." Mick grimaced and gripped his chair, wanting her out of his space.

"Methinks he doth protest too much," she replied, before turning and flouncing out of the cubby-hole he laughingly called his office.

For as long as Mick had worked security in this office block, twice a week, every week, at six-thirty in the morning, he'd watched the delivery van arrive at the barrier, via one of the cameras set in every corridor. In the past, he'd kept a vague eye on the man, making sure he followed his set route, before he returned to his book or current box set. However, for the last month, he'd been glued to his screens, watching the new man as he filled up the various vending machines and water coolers scattered around the eight-story building. Mick stared, following the man's every move, unable to tear himself away.

Now, after allowing enough time to make sure Ruby had gone, Mick returned to the monitors. He found his target once more. The man moved like a panther down the long corridors, careful and silent, with an obvious strength from the way he carried the huge water bottles as if they weighed nothing. The thought made Mick shiver. He didn't understand why this man should fascinate him so much. He didn't even know his name and new people usually unnerved him. The other cleaners left him alone. Only Ruby had persisted in her attempts to get him to talk.

'I need to keep focused on the cameras,' he'd told them when they tried to involve him in their lives. *'I don't drink, so there's no point in going to the pub.'* For every attempt, he'd come up with an excuse not to accept.

'You need to get your head out of your books once in a while,' Ruby had said more than once. But his books helped him to escape by providing worlds so different from his own.

Checking the monitors for reception revealed Ruby and Mary, another cleaner, talking to the man, but frustratingly, Mick couldn't hear what they said. Both peered up at the camera, and Mick glanced away, as if he were some Peeping Tom caught in the act. When he looked again, only the two women remained in view. He anxiously checked all the screens.

"So, this is where you are," a soft voice said out of nowhere. Surprised, Mick nearly fell out of his seat again. After collecting himself, he turned toward the door and saw the voice came from the man he'd been watching for the last few weeks.

"You shouldn't be here," he spluttered. "This isn't part of your route. You have to stick to your designated route, or it doesn't work."

"What doesn't work?" the man asked.

"Me making sure you do your job properly. I check you do the work and leave at the right time before I clock off. You'll be late now, and I've got to be out of here at seven on the dot. I can't be late waiting for you. It's important to keep to routines. If people don't follow the rules, it's dangerous. You know that." He shuffled papers on his desk, needing something to do with his hands.

"I'm sorry," the man said. "I didn't mean to upset you. Ruby said to introduce myself because we haven't met."

"Ruby should keep quiet," Mick muttered under his breath. The man didn't leave. Instead he grinned.

"You'll get no argument from me. I've noticed Ruby does like to gossip. Anyway, my name's Ceri, Ceri Llewellyn. Ruby said you're called Mick." He moved a few steps forward and held out his hand. Mick stared then pushed his chair backward until he hit the edge of a desk. Ceri halted when Mick didn't put his hand out in response.

"It's okay, I don't bite. If you don't want to shake my hand, it's fine. Not everyone does."

Mick's mother had taught him to be polite. He wiped his palm on his trouser leg and screwed up enough courage to hold up his right arm. The hand that shook his was dry and firm. Like the man, his fingers were long and thin. He wore rings on several of them.

"My name is Mick. Mick Flanagan. I've worked nights here for five years." He let go of Ceri. "Why is your hair green, and isn't Ceri a girl's name?"

Ceri cocked his head to one side. "Um, okay, I like a man who's straight to the point. My hair is green because I like to keep changing it. This week it's green. Next week it could be orange or purple or blue. It's the rainbow, you know, red and yellow and pink and green, orange and purple and blue. Like the song. You must know it."

Mick shook his head. Why would anyone make themselves stand out so much? His hair was auburn and curly. A beard covered most of his face. His mum had called him her little teddy bear before... He shook himself, not wanting to visit that memory.

"Are you all right? You shivered."

Mick sat up straight in his chair. "I'm fine. Why would you want to dye your hair every week all those different colors?"

"I like to be different, I suppose. Anyway, it's symbolic. You know, a rainbow representing all colors and all people, no matter what they are, black or white, young or old, gay or straight."

Is he gay? He can't be interested in me. Has Ruby said something? Does she know? The speed of his breathing increased. *Not now. Can't panic now.* He pulled at the elastic band on his wrist, willing the anxiety away. He needed to get Ceri out of his office.

"Are you sure you're okay? Can I get you some water? You've gone pale."

Mick desperately attempted to control his body and breathing. "I'm fine. Just tired. It's been a long night."

"You don't fancy getting breakfast somewhere, do you? There's a café around the corner. I could meet you there."

Mick wasn't sure he'd heard right. "What?"

Ceri remained too close. "Breakfast. You know — food. You must eat. This place does a great full English and the strongest tea. I'd say it'll put hairs on your chest, but you seem to have enough already."

Thoughts flew around his brain. What did this man want from him? Was this some sort of prank? Had Ruby made a bet with this man? Would they laugh at him if he said yes? Mick thought Ceri was even more beautiful in the flesh, with his bright blue eyes rimmed with black, pale pink lips and sharp cheekbones. He picked up his bag and began to pack away. To his horror, a ball of red wool fell out and rolled onto the floor. Ceri picked it up and held out his hand with a puzzled expression on his face.

"You knit?" he asked.

"So what?" Mick grabbed the ball and stuffed it back into the bag.

"Nothing," Ceri said. "Is it a *Doctor Who* scarf? I couldn't help noticing the box set."

"No. If you must know, I make hats for premature babies. The hospital likes to have them in certain colors. My mum taught me to knit when I was little, and it gives me something to do during the night."

"What a lovely thing to do." Ceri's expression had softened. "So, about breakfast?"

"I can't come with you. I've got to go shopping this morning. I always go to the supermarket on a Thursday before it gets busy," Mick explained. "I can't have breakfast with you either. You'd better go, or you'll be late. Please." He needed Ceri gone.

"Okay, maybe not today," Ceri said. "But that doesn't mean I'm giving up on you. I'll be back. I haven't been working this route for long, and it would be good to make a new friend." He swept out of the room before Mick could reply.

Minutes later, Mick watched Ceri get into his van. Relieved and puzzled in equal measure, he pulled his jacket from the back of his chair and put it on. Now, at least, he could leave. He slung his bag over his shoulder.

"Everything okay?" Fred asked, taking the empty seat Mick had vacated.

"Yes," Mick replied, succinctly.

"Good lad. I'll see you tonight then. I'm doing a double shift as Wilf is off today. You have a good day. Anything exciting planned?"

"Shopping." Mick liked Fred and Wilf. Neither expected him to converse much.

"Right—it's Thursday. Well, have a good time shopping."

The supermarket he used the same time every week was a fifteen-minute stroll away. Mick liked the early mornings except in the deepest winter. Now it was cold but dry. While he walked around the store, Mick thought about Ceri. He didn't get why Ceri should bother with him, and he still thought Ceri was a funny name for a man. No one talked to him while he shopped, except Marie on the till. He always went to the same till and bought the same things, then had breakfast. He liked routine. This way, he didn't have to make many decisions, unless they'd run out of something.

Ceri asking him to go to the café had unnerved him and reminded him of things he didn't want to think about, things he couldn't think about. Tears pricked the corners of his eyes and he glanced around, terrified someone would notice, but no one had. At the till, Marie smiled at him.

"Morning, Mick. Let's get this lot through, shall we? Same as ever, I see. Here, have one of these caramel eggs on me. Live dangerously for once."

"Thanks," he muttered as he packed the rest of the food away, unsure of what else to say. Then it was back to his flat and his memories of Alfie. He didn't think of him all the time anymore, but even though Alfie and Ceri were nothing alike, Ceri's sudden interest in him shared common ground with the first time he'd met Alfie.

Mick remembered the day so well. Blond, tall and proverbially handsome, Alfie had appeared in Mick's life like a guardian angel when he'd been hit by a car, thus proving his mother's view that the world outside their home was a dangerous place. Alfie, a paramedic, had picked him up from the pavement and treated him but, more surprisingly, had also turned up later to visit him in hospital.

'I brought you some grapes and something to read. The nurses said you'd had no visitors, and I didn't like to think of you here all by yourself.'

'My mum doesn't like hospitals,' he'd explained. *'She thinks they're full of sick people and their germs.'*

Alfie had smiled his beautiful smile and Mick's heart had missed several beats. After that, Alfie had visited every day.

'It's just you and her then,' Alfie had stated the next day, taking the seat next to Mick's bed. The warmth of Alfie's hand around his had made him feel safe. Maybe that was why he'd told Alfie everything.

'Yes. I don't know who my dad was. I don't even know if he's alive or dead. My mum said I was special – that she wanted me, *not some man. When I was old enough, she didn't want me to go to school and said she'd home school me, but someone reported her. I remember, on the first day, some kids laughed at me because of my long hair. I cut it off with scissors and made a right mess. I mostly liked school, despite the bullying, and I tried to keep my head down as much as possible. My life was home and school. I didn't make friends, except for Sally, who took me under her wing and was kind to me, but Mum never allowed her to visit. No one came into the house.'*

Throughout his speech, Alfie had kept hold of Mick's hand. He didn't say anything or explain why, so Mick talked and talked about his life. He was eighteen and unemployed. All he wanted to do was write stories.

'I'll bring you some paper.' Alfie couldn't have said any words that would have made him happier. He'd told him about his ideas and again Alfie had listened. He'd scribbled his thoughts down and read them out loud for Alfie. When he'd laughed, Mick had smiled and felt good inside. Within two weeks, he'd known he was absolutely and completely in love for the first time in his life, but with a man.

As soon as Mick had gotten home from the hospital, he'd told his mother about Alfie and how he felt about him. She'd freaked. Scared, he'd run out and called Alfie for help. They'd met in a local café.

'*She told me I was unnatural, and I'd get AIDs or something. She said I had to choose — you or her. What do I do, Alfie?*' Mick had poured out his feelings, unable to stop himself, then sat there hoping...well, just hoping. Although there had been other people in the café, Alfie had taken his hands, looked straight at him and wiped away a teardrop from his cheek.

'*I want you to come home with me now. I want you to live with me. You need to leave her, Mick. I know it will be hard, but if you love me as you say you do, you need to spread your wings.*'

Mick had gone back with him. That night, Alfie had slowly removed Mick's clothes and touched him all over, then made love to him and taught Mick how to make love back. They'd had three years together.

Chapter Two

Ceri opened then closed his mouth, stopping himself uttering the expletive on the tip of his tongue as he failed to complete his move yet again. He limped to the bench at the side of the skate park and rubbed his knee while other younger and more skilled skateboarders showed off their skills. He had to face it. After three years of giving everything to his sport, he simply wasn't good enough to turn professional. His next competition would be his last. Time to grow up and accept what his parents had told him for years. He picked up his board then limped back to his room in a shared house a few streets away. Once stripped, he collapsed onto his narrow bed and slept.

A few hours later, Ceri woke, rubbed his eyes and swung his long legs to sit on the edge of the bed. His knee twinged.

"Shower." At least at this time of day he wouldn't be fighting with the four others who lived in the house. Once clean and dressed, he opened his only cupboard to find it as empty as his stomach. He needed food. He decided on a full English while he could afford one, despite it being midday, and he knew just the café.

Molly's Place served great food at reasonable prices and it was near enough to his house not to have to use his pride and joy. The cost of petrol meant his bike often remained in the garage he shared with a couple of other bikers. If he couldn't persuade Mick to eat with him, perhaps he could interest him with a ride somewhere out of town. It had been a while since Ceri had gone anywhere.

Molly nodded at him when he pushed through the door. The café was popular with workers from offices in the local area, but only a few stayed to eat inside. "What can I get you today, Ceri?" she asked.

"I'm treating myself. Full English please, but no tomato, and a large flat white coffee. I'll park myself over here." He pulled out the latest *Doctor Who* magazine and settled in his seat to read.

"Hi."

Ceri dragged himself away from an interesting article he'd been saving on male companions and glanced up to see a woman staring at him.

"Hi. I'm Ruby, from the Grafton building. Just in case you've forgotten already. I...wondered... How did you get on with Mick?"

Molly brought his food.

"That looks good," Ruby said.

"Why don't you join me? Molly's food is awesome."

"I only came in for a bacon butty. Oh hell, why not treat myself? I'll have what he's got, please."

Molly grinned. "One full English coming up — coffee or tea?"

"Oh tea, please." She settled into the seat opposite. "*Doctor Who*, huh? Mick is such a fan. He watches episodes through the night. He's always got a box set."

"So I saw. I tried talking to him. He's so shy and introverted. I asked him to have breakfast with me and I've never seen anyone pale like he did. What's his story?" Despite everything, Ceri was now *more* interested in learning about Mick. He could hear his sister's voice talking about waifs and strays, but what the hell — in for a penny.

Ruby leaned forward as if someone might be listening. "According to Mary, Mick had this boyfriend who died a few years back. She only knows because she also cleans at the hospital and this bloke was a paramedic. Meningitis — went just like that." She clicked her fingers. "Mick's worked as a night-time guard for a while. Keeps himself to himself. I've only managed a few conversations with him. He seems lonely — like he needs a friend. We all need friends, don't we? Wow, that looks scrumptious."

Molly placed the plate on the table. "Enjoy."

Ruby sniffed the air. "There is no smell in the world as good as bacon."

Ceri nodded as he chewed then swallowed. "Maybe I'll try to talk Mick round again. I mean, who could resist my charms."

Ceri didn't have any real friends in Cheltenham, just acquaintances, since Dickhead had bailed on him — who the hell calls their son Richard when their surname is Headley? Bastard had got him to spend his savings during his gap year, said they'd be together while he studied, and Ceri tried to go professional as a skateboarder, and then buggered off. Sixth months into his first year, he'd met someone else, left Ceri high and dry, with little money and nowhere to live. Two years on, and with nothing to show for all his practice and ambition, Ceri had arrived at a crossroads and didn't know what to do with his life. Making friends with Mick was a start. People interested him. Perhaps it was time to throw in the towel and apply to university after all. His parents and sister would be over the moon. He sipped his coffee and turned his attention back to Ruby. "I could do with a real friend too."

"If you want, you could always come out with me and my friends. I know this bloke. He'd be perfect for you. We're crashing a university party on Saturday."

Ceri shook his head. "Nah, thanks for the offer. Money's tight, you know."

Ruby nodded. "I work three jobs — I know what you mean. But a girl's got to have fun when she can, and some of those university types are more interesting than the lads around here. Some like to flash the cash."

"Just be careful," Ceri said. *Yeah, just like I was.*

Ruby glanced up through her fringe. "Yes, Dad. Careful is my middle name. I've seen what can happen. I don't drink too much, and I don't do drugs."

"It's easy to make the wrong decisions. Have your head turned by a pretty face or sexy arse." Ceri sighed. "Sorry, I don't want to put a damper on your day. I'm at one of those crossroads in life, I guess, and you don't need to be brought down by my bad mood."

Ruby licked her lips and wiped her mouth with the paper napkin. "That was gorgeous. Now, in my mind, you can see your situation as an ending or a chance for a new beginning. My nanna says that, and she should know — she's on husband number three."

"Your nanna sounds like a wise woman."

Ruby stood. "See you soon. And if you change your mind about Saturday, give me a call." Ceri watched her go. *Let operation Mick commence.*

* * * *

Monday morning, dead on six-thirty, Ceri pulled up at the gate of Grafton House. All weekend, he'd thought about Mick and what he'd say to persuade him to go out. The rest of the time he'd spent at the skate park practicing mostly out of habit, but he'd finally decided what to do when his knee ached. The joy he usually felt at nailing each move had largely dissipated, especially when he watched teenagers effortlessly doing better. He pressed the buzzer, then smiled to himself at how ridiculously pleased he was to hear Mick tell him to come in. He unloaded the supplies into the small stock room and wheeled the first trolley load into the lift to begin stocking up the various machines.

As he wandered around, Ceri thought about Mick and why he was even trying to get to know him. Mick and his usual type were poles apart. Dickhead was tall and handsome with the broad shoulders of a swimmer, whereas Mick was shorter and stockier and had all that hair. *Definitely different.* He and Dickhead had met at school. Ceri had grown up in a small town on the Welsh border. His parents were teachers at the town's public school. Dickhead had been head boy, and they'd fucked like rabbits, spending the rest of their time discussing their futures together. *So much for that.*

He rolled his eyes, lifted his head, stared into the camera at the end of the corridor and waved, hoping it would make Mick smile. Why that should matter to him Ceri didn't know, but it did. When he finished his round, he headed to Mick's office.

"Morning," he said cheerfully, leaning against the door jamb, keeping his voice light. "Good weekend?" Mick glanced up, and Ceri noticed the slightest of curls each side of his mouth. He wanted to high-five himself. Had a faint light of hope switched on at the end of the tunnel? Maybe Mick was interested in him after all.

"You dyed your hair a different color," Mick said. Ceri noted that he didn't tell him anything about how he'd spent the weekend. "It looks good orange. It suits you. Did *you* do anything interesting this weekend?"

Hmm, he's positively chatty this morning but still deflected a question with a question. "No, not really, just practicing."

"For what?" Mick asked.

"I skateboard. I'm hoping to do better in this year's county championships, though it'll be my last. You ever skateboarded?" Ceri asked.

Mick shook his head. "My mother would never have allowed me to do anything so dangerous. Are you any good?"

Strange comment. But Ceri didn't ask. "I'm good, but I don't think I'm good enough to win anything. The championship is a final try then say goodbye sort of thing. You should come and watch me practice. Maybe have a go yourself."

"I'm no good at anything sporty," Mick said. His eyes showed such sadness. "I used to avoid gym if I could. TV was more my thing. Ever watched *Doctor Who*?"

From the expression on Mick's face, Ceri guessed this question mattered. He carefully considered his answer. "I may have watched a few, now and again—

you know when nothing else was on. So, who's your favorite Doctor then?" *Now this was something they could talk about.* Mick was balling his hand into a fist and Ceri wondered why.

"My favorite is Tom Baker, the Fourth Doctor," Mick replied tersely.

"Oh, he's one of the old ones, isn't he? The one with the long scarf and the jelly babies. I quite liked Matt Smith. He's a lot like the Second Doctor."

Mick's hand unfurled. "You know about the Second Doctor?"

Ceri nodded. "He played the recorder, didn't he?" Mick rewarded his comment with a shy smile. "My favorite Doctor is the Ninth. He was all dark and brooding in that leather coat with his northern accent. I wish he'd done more than one series. I bet you thought I'd say the Tenth because everyone likes him."

"It crossed my mind," Mick replied. His smile now reached his brown eyes. "And how come you know about the Second Doctor?"

"I said I'd seen a few episodes. I happen to like *War Games,* and who could resist Jamie in a kilt, although my favorite companion is…"

"Captain Jack Harkness," they said in unison.

"Oh yeah," Ceri said wistfully. "I could do bad things with him." Sensing he was on a roll, he ventured, "Come have breakfast with me, Mick. I'm starving, and we could talk *Doctor Who* some more."

"You look like you could do with a square meal," Mick joked. Ceri sensed he'd relaxed now he knew Ceri was a real fan of his favorite show.

"What? I'm naturally skinny. My sister hates me because I eat like a horse and don't put on any weight.

Skateboarding is good exercise. I could meet you down in the loading bay," he finished.

The smiling eyes disappeared. "No, I can't. I've things to do. Monday is washing day. I've the bedding to do. Alfie always…"

"You couldn't give it a miss, just this once."

Mick started packing his bag, hunched over, almost folding in on himself. "No, Monday is washing day." He glanced at his watch. "You need to go, now. I have to make sure you're out of the building. Please, or you'll make me late and I mustn't be late."

"Okay, but don't think I won't keep asking. We all need a break sometimes. I'll be back later in the week."

"It's fine," Mick replied. "You don't need to bother with me. I'm fine. You, you…"

Ceri turned. "I want to hear about your favorite episode next time," he said over his shoulder, then pushed his trolley down the corridor.

* * * *

"Me again," Ceri said, a couple of days later. This time Mick had obviously expected him and greeted him at the door. An aroma of coffee filled the air.

"That smells good," he said sniffing. "It's brass monkeys out there this morning. I could do with something warm inside me before I go out again." Mick's expression didn't change. "Do you have any to spare?"

Mick lifted his thermos. "I'll pour some into the little cup. I don't have another mug."

"That's great. Thank you." Ceri took the cup and breathed in the taste first. "This isn't cheap stuff," he said.

"I have a machine at home that grinds beans."

Ceri sipped. "Hmm, that's smooth. So, did you think about your favorite episode," he said.

"What's yours?" Mick asked. "Then I'll tell you mine."

Ceri had thought long and hard about his choice. Should he go for a fan favorite like *The Caves of Androzani* or tell the truth? "You might find my choice strange, but I have a real soft spot for *Boom Town*. I think it asks questions about life and death, and I like how it's filmed in Cardiff and Jack's in it too... I've never been to Cardiff Bay. Have you?"

"No, I haven't. They do tours, don't they?" Mick's face, what Ceri could see of it, lit up when he talked about *Doctor Who*. It warmed Ceri's heart to see it. An idea came to him but now wasn't the time. He still wanted to get Mick to go to the café with him.

"*Boom Town* is a different choice. My favorite is *Genesis of the Daleks*."

"Another one that asks questions about life and death," Ceri said. "Perhaps we should think of a fun one as well over breakfast. We could go to this place I know."

"Hello, you two. Running late, aren't you, Ceri? Morning, Mick."

Mick stood. "Wilf, sorry. You should go, Ceri. It's after the end of my shift." He grabbed at his things, quickly gathering everything, and threw his bag over his shoulder.

"I'll walk out with you," Ceri said.

"No, I need to talk to Wilf, tell him what's happened overnight. I'll see you next time."

"All right, if that's what you want." Ceri nodded at Wilf who glanced between them and once more pushed his trolley back to the entrance of the building. There was always next time.

Chapter Three

Mick couldn't understand why he kept asking. Twice a week Ceri delivered to the building and twice a week, over the last four weeks, he'd asked Mick out. "He'll keep asking," Ruby said. "I've been to the café he talks about and the breakfasts are delicious. Why don't you go? Who would it hurt? Alfie's been gone a long time now."

Mick had wanted to shout at her. What did she know? Alfie had been his life. He couldn't let himself feel anything for anyone — not again — and yet... Seeing Ceri, hearing his voice, made him smile inside.

"So, what you watching today? Doesn't look like *Doctor Who* to me."

Mick looked up to see Ceri leaning nonchalantly against the door. His hair remained the same orange color but he'd tied it back so Mick could see each ear had several piercings. Ceri's T-shirt and trousers clung to his body like a second skin. Butterflies fluttered in Mick's stomach. No one since Alfie had made him react this way. He didn't understand it. Ceri was nothing like

Alfie. He was narrow where Alfie had been broad, of average height when Alfie had been tall, graceful whereas Alfie had been more like a bull in a china shop, and Ceri was younger than him, whereas Alfie had been older. Mick had always felt small in his arms, so protected, and above all safe. He couldn't imagine that with Ceri. It was a total cliché, but Alfie had taken care of him, and he didn't think Ceri was the looking-after type, but he lingered there, still smiling, and that Mick couldn't ignore.

"It's *Angel,* series two. I've watched *Buffy* already, so I figured I'd continue through," Mick said, pressing the pause button.

Somehow, Ceri slid his hand into his trouser pocket. "Yum, Spike was so handsome. Those cheekbones could cut glass. I always preferred him to Angel. I guess I like bad boys too much! What do you think? Spike or Angel?"

And there it was. Ceri telling him he liked men, making it crystal clear, putting it out there for Mick to process. How he answered could make all the difference. What should he say? Had Ruby told Ceri about Alfie? Did he already know? He'd already mentioned he liked the omnisexual Captain Jack Harkness. *Do I know how I feel?* There'd been no one else but Alfie. *Do I want Ceri to go away or try harder to get my attention*?

"I liked Spike's coat," Mick said, choosing a neutral topic.

"Yeah, what is it with men and their swishy coats in sci-fi programs? Are you more of a *Buffy* fan then?" Ceri asked, still obviously fishing. Mick thought for a moment before answering.

"No," he said, taking a breath to settle his nerves. "I always preferred Giles."

"Hmm. Interesting," Ceri replied.

Before he could continue, Mick interrupted, "You'd better get finished. The clock is ticking." Heat spread across his face.

Ceri smirked. "In a hurry to get rid of me then. Maybe next week I'll ask you out to breakfast again, and you can tell me why you like Anthony Head so much."

"Well, you do look like you could do with a square meal," Mick joked.

Ceri sensed he'd relaxed now he knew Ceri was a real fan of his favorite show.

"What? I'm naturally skinny. My sister, Megan — did I mention I have a twin sister? She hates me because I can eat like a horse and don't put on any weight. I don't intend to give up asking, you know."

With that, Ceri sauntered away down the corridor, whistling to himself. He moved like a cat, his limbs long and lithe. At the corner, he glanced over his shoulder and blew a kiss. Mick's insides did a flip. Maybe next time Ceri asked, he'd say yes.

"That lad Ceri seems nice," Wilf said, when Mick handed over the night shift. "Ruby said he asked you out to breakfast. You should go. Live a little. I heard you talking about *Doctor Who* with him. If he likes your favorite show, he can't be bad. Would it hurt to give him a chance? You're too young to waste your life on your own, even if you're only friends."

Mick nodded. Wilf had a point. He *was* lonely and Ceri seemed kind. And, he *did* like *Doctor Who*.

The next time Ceri delivered to his building, Mick waited with his heart in his mouth. He'd tidied the office over and over. This time when Ceri asked, he intended to say yes. Ten minutes later, Ceri was there, strolling down the corridor, smiling at the camera.

Mick wiped his hands on his trousers. His throat felt drier than the Sahara.

"Morning, Mick. And how are you today? The sun is due to shine, I'm told. It's likely to be a perfect day for a breakfast out. Would you like to —"

"Yes," Mick croaked, without meeting Ceri's gaze. He couldn't manage that much — not yet.

"Sorry. Did you say yes?"

Now, Mick looked up. "I did. Is that okay? You meant it, didn't you?" What if it had all been a joke after all and now Ceri would laugh at him? He noticed Ceri had deep blue eyes. He'd never allowed himself to gaze for so long before. Ceri took a step forward.

"Of course I meant it. I'm just surprised is all. I'll meet you in twenty minutes down in the parking bay by my van. Is that all right? I'll get off before you change your mind."

Mick nodded. "I can eat what I want, can't I?" But Ceri was already on his way out.

* * * *

"Aren't we going straight to the café?" Mick asked, when they drove past the place Ceri had mentioned.

"Not yet, I've got to drop the van off at the depot first. You'll be all right on the back of my bike, won't you? It's not far, and I've a spare helmet in my locker."

"You drive a motorbike," Mick replied. *I can't go on one of them. I'll fall off. I'll break something.* He shifted in his seat, pulling nervously at the seat belt with his shaking hand. "I've never been on one. Aren't they dangerous? They always seem to be crashing them on all the TV hospital shows I've seen. I could get a bus, or we could go back, and you could drop me off at the café. Yes, that's best. It won't take long to turn around and drop me off. I don't want to cause an accident riding behind you." Mick swore his heart was ready to burst out of his chest. *Stay calm. Don't panic. Please don't let him see you like this.* He grabbed the edge of the seat while attempting to control his breathing.

Ceri reached over and briefly touched his leg. "Hey, don't worry. I'm a good driver. I've passed the advanced test. I couldn't carry a passenger otherwise, and it's only a short distance. You can hang on to me. I won't mind. Come on, you're going to the café, live a little bit more. And you haven't seen me in full leathers."

Ceri's words and wide smile settled the butterflies enough for Mick to nod. Ceri wouldn't hurt him. He didn't know why, but this was one thing he was sure about. Ceri had been nothing but kind.

At the depot, Ceri parked the van and disappeared into the building, leaving Mick waiting at the entrance. He stood watching the people come and go until the sound of a roaring engine made him turn. A figure dressed in black leather pulled up on the bike in front of him, parked it and swung his leg over to stand in front of the gleaming machine. He lifted his visor.

"What d'you think? Isn't she gorgeous?" Ceri reached into the back, took out another helmet and offered it to Mick.

Mick scanned Ceri from head to toe. Suddenly, the room in his pants diminished as his cock sprang to life. Stunned, he couldn't find words so took the helmet and stared at it then glanced up, wide-eyed and weak at the knees at the sight in front of him. *Oh God, when did I get a thing for men in leather?* He didn't understand why this man affected him so much. He hadn't so much as looked at another man before or after Alfie. Somehow,

Ceri had got him out of his routine, and now he wanted to get him on the back of a bike.

"Ready?" Ceri asked. "I'll get on first, and you get on behind me. Put your arms around my waist and hold on. I won't go too fast."

Mick nodded. It felt awkward clasping Ceri, but Mick could reach all the way around and grab his other hand.

"Comfortable?" Ceri asked.

"As I can be."

"If you like it enough, we'll get you the right clothes to wear as well."

Surprised at himself, Mick found he was less worried with his arms around Ceri as he wove the powerful machine through the morning traffic to the cafe. The sensation of movement, the wind on his body and the throb of the engine left him feeling exhilarated, so much so, when they stopped after ten minutes, he felt disappointed.

"Okay?" Ceri asked him when they arrived. "I didn't go too fast for you?"

"No," Mick replied, letting Ceri go and swinging his leg over the back of the bike. He removed his helmet. "I enjoyed it more than I expected."

Ceri grinned at him. "We'll make a biker of you yet."

Once inside, Mick selected a table at the back of the room, out of the way.

"Choose what you want," Ceri said. "I asked you, so it's on me. I'm having the full English without tomatoes. I can't stand them. So, what do you want?"

Mick stared at the menu. There were so many things to choose from. He had no idea what to do. How did he choose? It was Monday—on Mondays he had cornflakes and a mug of tea. They had cereals on the menu. He'd have his usual.

"I'll have cornflakes and tea," he said.

Ceri frowned. Mick clasped the menu. Had he said something wrong? He wasn't used to eating out. Alfie had always chosen where they went and what they ate.

"It's all right," Ceri said. "I worked two extra shifts this week so I can afford it if you want more. At least have something hot. A bacon butty, or are you a vegetarian? Sorry, I didn't think. They do great omelets here with lots of flavors."

Mick didn't know what to say. Ceri had clearly misunderstood. "I'm not a vegetarian. It's just it's Monday." He stopped. Ceri would think he was mad. He wouldn't understand it was easier to buy small packets of cereal and eat them over the week. Each variety pack had six packets. On Thursday, when he shopped, he bought breakfast at the supermarket and had a bacon sandwich with his mug of tea. *That's it*. He could adjust his routine and have the cornflakes on Thursday, couldn't he? He breathed a sigh of relief.

"All right," he said. "I'll have a bacon butty and tea — breakfast tea. I like it strong."

"Good." Ceri smiled at his comment and went to the counter to order.

When he returned, they talked more about *Doctor Who* and found he and Ceri agreed about so much. The food arrived quickly. Mick bit into his roll, savoring the salty taste of the bacon.

"Good, huh?" Ceri said.

Mick nodded and licked his lips, suddenly conscious of Ceri staring at him. "I wasn't sure at first about a female Doctor," Mick admitted, starting the conversation again.

"I thought it was brave and about time," Ceri replied. "I liked her outfit."

"The episodes were a bit mixed, but I'm looking forward to the next series.

"Have you ever been to a convention?" Ceri asked. "There's one in Cardiff next weekend I'm going to. There's a bus tour of the area with locations, and I want to go to Ianto's shrine and see the water tower. I assume you watched *Torchwood* as well, if you're a Jack fan..." He stopped talking, as though not sure what to say next.

"What?" Mick asked, unsure of the expression in Ceri's face.

"Why don't we both go to Cardiff?" Ceri pulled his phone out of his jacket. "I could check if there are any more tickets. I was planning to drive there and back in a day, but we could stay at a cheap B&B overnight, or at one of those lodge places and have a look around. Being on a bike makes it easier. If we stayed two nights, we could go to Cardiff Bay. Shame the *Doctor Who* Exhibition closed, but there are other places. What d'you think?" He tapped at his phone. "Yes, there are a few tickets left."

Mick hurriedly swallowed the last bite of his roll despite the lump in his throat. He gripped the edge of the table. A mixture of excitement and fear bubbled up in him. His eyes darted from side to side. He hadn't been outside Cheltenham for years, not since Alfie. He'd done nothing since Alfie. He struggled to control the rising panic, and just about kept his breathing under control. Could he do this? Little else would tempt him, but going to Cardiff Bay and all the other places he'd only seen on the screen, that was so... He felt a hand touch his arm.

"Mick, are you all right? You started to breathe funny."

"I'm fine. Sorry, I get anxiety attacks." No one was more surprised than him to hear those words come from his mouth.

"Oh. Don't worry. It was only a suggestion," Ceri said. "We don't have to go, but I would like to get to know you more."

"Why?" Mick asked, more harshly than he meant to. "Why me? I'm nothing special. I'm not even good-looking, like you."

"You think I'm good-looking?" Ceri asked. "Most people think I'm a little outlandish. Haven't you noticed people staring at us? My black leathers and bright hair get strange looks."

Mick straightened in his chair and glanced around. The truth was, he hadn't noticed. He'd been so absorbed talking to Ceri, he hadn't been aware of anyone else. For him, there had been no one in the room but the man in front of him. Could he do this? Maybe it was time to find out, and he longed to go to Cardiff. He had his anxiety medication. This would be a test. He took a deep breath.

"Okay, get me a ticket. I can give you the money for it," he said, trying not to think about what he was agreeing to. "I'll do some research online and book us in somewhere. One of those motels would be better. They're less conspicuous. There'll be more than one in Cardiff." He breathed, having got the words out. Now he'd said it out loud, he would have to do it. He couldn't go back on his word. Ceri rewarded him with a smile that made his heart melt. He yawned. "I'd better get going. I need some sleep. I'll see you Thursday morning, won't I? I'll sort everything out. Can you give me a lift home, then you'll know where to pick me up on Friday?"

"Sure."

Mick directed Ceri to a stylish block of flats on the outskirts of the town center. All he could think about was the decision he'd made.

"We're going to do this, aren't we?" he said, taking off the helmet.

Ceri dismounted and stowed the helmet in the box under the seat. "I hope so. Don't go changing your mind on me."

"You didn't answer my question about why me," Mick reminded him.

"You interest me, and we sci-fi fans have to stick together, don't we? Also, I've wanted to do this for a while." He leaned down and kissed Mick—just lightly and not for long. "Was that all right? Sorry, I should have asked. Your beard is softer than I expected."

A stunned Mick nodded and ran his hand across his face. He'd let it grow. Alfie had insisted he shaved and waxed. "You surprised me, that's all. People don't kiss me. It was…nice."

Ceri put his hand on Mick's arm, and Mick stared at those long fingers with their red-painted nails. He wanted Ceri to kiss him again. He craved simple human contact after being so long alone. It was a small gesture but meant a lot. He lifted his head and met Ceri's gaze.

"I'll see you Thursday morning. I'll ring you if I need to. Your number will be on file. We keep contact numbers in case of emergencies," he said, turning to take the stairs two at a time. At the top he turned and waved. Ceri was already astride the bike, ready to go. He revved the engine and roared off down the street.

Tears pricked at Mick's eyes, like some great flood was trying to release itself. A simple kiss had set off a chain reaction. His stomach churned. His hands shook. He swallowed down a lump in his throat. There was something special about the man he'd kissed, and now he desperately wanted more. Somehow, in the space of a few hours, he'd gone from breakfast to organizing a trip which involved staying overnight in a hotel. Was it the chance to visit all those places he'd only seen on TV, or the chance to spend more time with Ceri? For the next couple of days, he told himself the same message over and over.

You can do this.
You need to do this.
You want to do this.
You will do this.

Chapter Four

"You appear to have everything covered," Ceri said when they met again on Thursday morning, after examining at the paperwork Mick had put together. "You must let me give you money for the hotel booking. We can sort out the rest when we get there. I've borrowed some leathers which should fit you okay and keep you safe." What Ceri could see of Mick's face paled.

"You have passed your test to carry passengers on a motorway, haven't you?" Mick asked warily.

Ceri grinned. "Yes, of course I have. I did my advanced driving test a while back. It helped me get this job. And I'd never put anyone in danger. You'll be fine. Just hold on tight to me." This time Mick's skin turned a darker shade of pink. *I shouldn't tease him.* "I'll pick you up from your flat at eleven tomorrow. I can only fit a limited amount of stuff on the bike so don't go mad. You can fit a couple of layers under the leathers and…" He hesitated, uncertain how Mick would be about eating in a restaurant. "And perhaps a smart shirt and a pair of trousers so we could eat out. There are some good restaurants in the city. You are all right about going out to dinner with me, aren't you?"

Mick nodded. "As long as it's not too posh. I never know what to eat. I like pasta though."

"Then we can check out the Italian places." Ceri leaned forward, cupped Mick's cheek and kissed him. Mick made a sound like a gentle sigh and didn't pull away. Heat pooled in Ceri's chest. "I'm so excited, especially now I won't be on my own. It'll be good to have someone to obsess with. We should have hired costumes. Maybe next time." He glanced at his watch. "I'd better get off. Until tomorrow. I'll be lucky to sleep tonight."

"Me too," Mick replied. "I'm not used to it. After I've been shopping, I usually go straight to bed, but I want to stay awake for as long as I can, so I sleep tonight. Even so, I'll probably be up early and pacing the floor waiting for you."

Ceri hurried down the corridor, pushing his trolley into the lift. When the doors opened, Wilf stood waiting. He touched Ceri's arm. "You'll take care of him, won't you? Treat him well. He's a good man. I don't want you playing with his emotions."

"I'm not," Ceri assured him. "I know what it's like to be on the receiving end. We're just two *Doctor Who* fans having a weekend away. Anything else is up to Mick." Wilf nodded and pressed for the lift to return. In just over twenty-four hours, they'd be away.

* * * *

It was a bit of a squash, but they fitted everything into the bike's various compartments. When Mick pulled the leathers over his clothes, Ceri whistled.

"They suit you. You'd look like a Hell's Angel if you had a ponytail to go with your beard." Intending to kiss him again, Ceri moved closer, but Mick backed up to the wall, darting his gaze left and right. Ceri stopped, not wanting to crowd him. He needed to change the subject. Tentatively, he reached out and touched Mick's face. This time he didn't back away.

"Sorry, I didn't mean to spook you. I should have thought. Hmm, I wonder what you look like under all this hair?" he whispered. "I'm good at shaving. Perhaps I can alter it slightly so I can see more of you." Mick's eyes widened before he lowered his head. It had been a while since Ceri had shaved anyone else, but the idea of being so close to Mick aroused him. The act would be so intimate, so sensuous.

"Perhaps," Mick replied, his skin pinking again. He looked up and finally met Ceri's gaze. "And maybe you could dress like the Tenth Doctor for me."

Ceri burst out laughing. "Don't tell me you really have a kink for swishy coats. Is there anything else I should know, as we'll be sharing a room tonight?" Mick shook his head.

"Well, I'm game if you are. We could check out the charity shops. You never know what they might have." Mick returned Ceri's grin and visibly relaxed now they'd shared some secrets.

The journey to Cardiff took just over ninety minutes. Mick held on tightly to Ceri's waist the whole way down the M5 and M4 motorways. They followed the signs to Cardiff Bay, parked the bike, stashed their leather trousers and made their way to the water tower.

The place was full of people, wandering around, checking out the sights. Ceri dug his phone from his pocket and took photographs of them both at the tower, at Ianto's shrine, at the church and leaning against the rails in front of the water. His stomach rumbled.

"I know it's the wrong time to eat, but I'm starving," he said. "Burger all right to tide us over?"

Mick nodded without reply. He did a three-hundred-and-sixty-degree turn. "I can't believe I'm here. It's incredible seeing everything for real. I'll wait for you over there, if that's all right. It's where Jack sat with Ianto." He pointed at the steps that surrounded the open area.

"I won't be long." Ceri quickly bought the burgers, hoping Mick would like onions. He handed the box to Mick and sat next to him.

"The bike journey was great," Mick said. "I thought I'd be more scared, but it was exhilarating. This is good too."

Lots of people milled around, many dressed in costume, obviously *Doctor Who* or *Torchwood* fans intending like them to go to the convention the next day. Ceri lifted his face toward the sun. The heat warmed his face, but there was also a breeze coming off the water. "I'd like to come back here again when we've more time. Maybe eat at the café over there. You know, the one in *Boom Town*. Or we could take a boat trip round the bay." He bit into the burger again and wiped juice from his mouth. They ate in silence for a while, taking in the view.

"I'd love to come back here with you," Mick said, gazing at him with soft eyes.

Ceri returned his gaze for a few moments. Needing to do something, he wiped his face with a paper napkin and stood up. "Over there is where the TARDIS parked," he said, pointing across the paved amphitheater. "You know where Jack ran across from the Torchwood Hub and dived onto it."

"And there's the rail where they stood at the end of the Face of Boe speech," Mick continued. "I expect we could do this all day."

Ceri nodded and held out his hand to pull Mick to his feet. "You're right, but we'd better go to the hotel and book in. I'm getting sweaty in this leather jacket. I'll ring the restaurant as well and see if we can book for tomorrow night."

Thirty minutes later, they were sitting in their room. Mick had immediately taken the sofa, so Ceri spread himself out on the bed. It was a big bed, more than big enough for two people with a space in between.

"Fancy a coffee?" Mick said. "It's probably lousy, but the tea's likely to be worse. Or I could get us something to drink from the machine."

"Coffee's fine," Ceri replied. Now they were together, alone in a bedroom, it suddenly seemed more real. He watched as Mick made the coffee then motioned for him to sit by his side.

"Is it okay if I kiss you?" Ceri asked.

"You haven't asked before," Mick responded. "And, yes, I like it when you kiss me. I'm out of practice. It's been three years since…"

Ceri leaned in and kissed him. This time, he wrapped his hands behind Mick's back and pulled him in. Tentatively, he pushed his tongue forward and traced across Mick's teeth until Mick opened fully, and tongue met tongue. Mick smelled good this close and his beard tickled. Ceri kissed down Mick's chin to his throat and neck. Gratified to hear the other man groan, he brought one hand around and placed it on his chest before slowly moving down. He pulled the zip of Mick's jeans and heard his breath hitch in panic.

"It's okay," Ceri whispered softly. "Let me do this for you. I want to, and I think you want me to as well." He slid down onto his knees and reached into Mick's jeans. Mick's hand rested on his shoulder and Ceri sensed his fear and confusion. "Please," he said.

Mick stared down at Ceri's eyes. Was that desire he saw there? Alfie had never done this, never been on his knees in front of *him*. It had always been Mick's role in their relationship. Alfie had fucked his mouth, and Mick had learned to deep throat without gagging. The prospect of being on the receiving end was strange, but his cock showed definite signs of interest. Ceri's hand lightly gripped Mick's erection. Instinctively, he pushed his hips upward, wanting more, loving the feeling of those smooth fingers massaging his bare skin. He could only imagine what it would be like to be taken into the warm, wet heat of Ceri's mouth. Finally, Ceri pulled Mick's cock free of his briefs. It bounced upward and stood proud. Embarrassment caused heat to rush to his face, but he couldn't help himself. He stared at the ceiling, scared to meet Ceri's gaze, afraid of what he might see. Moments later, a tongue gently caressed the tip of his shaft.

"You taste good," Ceri said. "I want you so much."

Mick allowed himself a brief glance downward. He gripped the sheets on either side of him, and he nodded, unsure of what words to use. He was sitting, fully dressed, in a hotel room, with a gorgeous man asking to suck his cock and he wasn't even dreaming.

He leaned back, closed his eyes and let the other man go to work.

Ceri took a deep breath before taking Mick's full length into his mouth and nuzzling the hair surrounding his cock. He did it over and over until Mick thought he could bear no more. He groaned and clutched at Ceri's head, threading his fingers through his hair. Ceri didn't stop. Instead, he wrapped a fist around the base of the shaft, applied his tongue to the head and delved into the slit. Mick knew he was leaking, but Ceri sucked it all up greedily, then licked a stripe along the vein underneath. Mick's cock strained toward him, begging for more, as if it had a mind of its own.

Mick clasped Ceri's hair between his fingers. "So close," he warned. He expected Ceri to pull away, but instead, he kept sucking as Mick exploded and poured into him. His whole body centered on the experience. Ceri milked him until nothing remained. Mick fought to keep himself together. He wanted to scream and cry. He wanted to pull Ceri up from his knees and hold him and never ever let him go. He wanted to fight any other man who tried to come near him. Instead, he sat up and stared down at the most unbelievable sight he'd ever seen. Ceri's eyes shone with tears. His lips were red and swollen, but there wasn't a hint of sadness in his face, only joy. Mick pulled him up to kiss him. He tasted himself on those lips. He had no words except, "Thank you."

"My pleasure," Ceri replied. He stood then sat next to Mick on the bed. "I love giving head. I'm told I'm good at it."

All at once, words tumbled out of Mick's mouth, words he'd never said to anyone. "His name was Alfie.

We had three years together. He looked after me then he died. In an instant, he was gone. It was three years ago. There's been no one since then, no one until you. I thought maybe I wouldn't feel the same again, and I'd died as well. I learned to cope by keeping my life in order, making every day the same, then you came along with your smile and your multi-colored hair, and changed everything. To be honest, I feel rather lost and confused, but more excited than I've felt in such a long time. I hope you'll give me time to get used to whatever this is." He breathed out.

Ceri smiled at him, stroked his face and stilled his shaking hands by taking them in his. For a little while, Ceri held his gaze until Mick's breathing returned to normal. Finally, he cupped Mick's cheek and spoke. "I'll give you whatever you want."

Chapter Five

Mick told Ceri everything. Once the floodgates opened, he couldn't stop. They sat next to each other on the bed with Ceri holding his hand. Mick couldn't look at Ceri. Instead he stared at the window and let the words flow. To begin, he told him about his mother and how she'd rejected him after he fell in love with Alfie.

"I'm not even sure it was because he was another man. She just refused to forgive me for leaving her. You see, I was all she had, all she'd ever had. She said I'd betrayed her, that I needed to make a choice. I chose him. He'd inherited the flat from his grandmother. He went out to work, and I stayed at home. I read, wrote my stories and watched television. I could watch my programs during the day, then I cooked us dinner and kept things tidy. Alfie liked everything kept a certain way. We'd go out to eat and sometimes to clubs. Alfie enjoyed dancing, and I liked to watch him. He'd flirt a bit, but he usually came home with me. He told me he would always come back to me, no matter how it looked, and he did." Mick shifted position on the bed, allowing the blood to flow back into his straightened leg. "I was content. Then my world came crashing down. Meningitis stole him from me. He died in a few hours."

Ceri squeezed his hand. "That must have been so hard. I can't begin to think how I'd have coped."

Mick held tight to Ceri's fingers, needing the anchor they gave him as tears fell down his cheeks. "I didn't know what to do at first. The world seemed so huge and confusing. At least his family was good to me. Then I found Alfie had left me the flat in his will. He'd looked after me beyond the grave. I had somewhere to live, but no income. Eventually, his sister got me the security guard job. Her husband runs the company, and I've worked in the Grafton Building ever since. Usually, I only talk to the cleaners and Wilf and Fred, but then you came along and threw my world into chaos. And this is the most I've said to anyone in years." He swallowed hard, needing to summon his courage again.

"You don't have to tell me anything else," Ceri said. "Your past isn't any of my business. The only thing that matters is the here and now." Ceri moved to kneel on the floor in front of him. He lifted a hand and wiped a tear from Mick's face. Mick braved meeting Ceri's gaze. Those beautiful blue eyes stared at him. He gripped the edge of the bed.

"You say that, Ceri, but the thing is, well, I don't get why you're interested in me. You've clearly been around." He paused, realizing what he'd said. "Sorry. I didn't mean that how it sounded. I meant you've had more experience of life and people than me."

Ceri shrugged. "If you're calling me a slut, Mick, you're probably right. There was a time when I didn't care—"

Mick frowned at him. "Don't say that. I hate it when people call themselves names. Too many other people in life are ready to call you names, so you shouldn't do it yourself. I wouldn't blame anyone trying it on with you—you're so pretty. I'm sorry if my description is wrong. I've never been good explaining my thoughts out loud. I've always been better writing things down. I don't get why someone who looks like you should want to be with me. I'm short and hairy. Alfie used to call me Frodo, after the hobbit from *Lord of the Rings*."

"I'm going to make us tea," Ceri said. "Then we can talk some more if you want. It's up to you."

Mick stood. "Tea would be great. I need the loo."

In the bathroom, Mick sat on the toilet, staring at the wall. Where had all those words come from and why had he told Ceri? As he'd said them, he'd experienced feelings of guilt. Over the last few months, after talking to Wilf, he'd wondered if Alfie had been the man he'd thought he was. Wilf had left a newspaper article open on their desk about people who controlled others. Had Alfie done that to him? He wiped more tears from his eyes. He didn't want to think about Alfie now. He needed to move on with his life. All he had to do was find the courage to put the past behind him.

Ceri guessed Mick needed a little time on his own. He had no illusions about his actions. He understood himself only too well. Perhaps studying psychology had helped him, or he'd spent too much time talking to himself since leaving home. He knew he was no alpha male, but if he wanted sex, he had it. He'd never fucked anyone—he'd never wanted to, but he knew he could be a toppy bottom. His parents might have despaired at his choices, but they'd never made him choose. The kettle boiled, and he poured the water onto the bags in the mugs.

He'd always liked a good time, but recently, he'd begun to feel too old to be having sex in back alleys and toilets, without the benefit of an introduction. He threw the soggy teabags into the bin and added milk to the cups and stirred as Mick emerged from the bathroom. Ceri grinned at him and was rewarded with a slight smile. Maybe what he needed now was someone he could share his life with—someone who needed more from him.

"What?" Mick asked, taking the proffered mug and sitting on the bed once more.

Ceri picked up his own drink and sat on the chair opposite rather than the floor. "For someone who supposedly isn't good with words, you've said a fair few. You say you're nothing special, but I disagree." He leaned forward and cupped Mick's cheek. "Truth is, I've not met anyone like you before, and I enjoy talking to you. I've been drifting around and doing nothing with my life." He stopped for a moment, then smirked. "Oh, and you've got a great cock. What more could a man ask for?"

Mick's cheeks flushed red under his beard, and he dropped his chin. Ceri lifted his face with one finger. He chuckled. "Well, you *do* have a great cock, and I hope to get up close and personal with it again, but not now. Let's finish these drinks, get out of here and have some fun. Barry Island's not far from here. We can play on the arcades and watch the sunset over the sea. My family used to go to the Island when we were kids. The main beach is huge, and since *Gavin and Stacey*, they even have tours of the area."

"I'd like that," Mick replied. "But how do we get there if it's an island?"

"Oh, it's not an actual island. It was once upon a time, but then they built the docks and a causeway to connect it to the mainland. There used to be a big holiday camp there, but it's all gone now. It also used to be the place where trains went to die." Mick looked puzzled so Ceri explained.

"They used to send old scrapped locomotives there — hundreds of them. My dad used to go regularly. He loves old steam trains. They left them there to rust. There's a funfair too that has new rides including a big wheel like the London Eye, and they've done up the promenade. Come on." He stood and held out his hand to Mick. "Let's get going. I can practically smell those fish and chips."

The main holiday season was still to come, and they were past the first glut of tourists who came at Easter, so Barry Island had only a few visitors. The funfair was open, but neither of them fancied going on the bigger rides.

"I get sick," Mick said, gazing up at the big wheel. "What about the dodgems?"

They spent time chasing each other around, bumping into different cars and laughing. After, they played the machines in the arcades and lost most of the money they put in. Mick spent ages trying to make the coins topple in the waterfall machine.

Ceri leaned over his shoulder, wrapped his arms around Mick's waist and laughed. "They glue them on you know, so they won't fall."

"Now you're teasing me, aren't you?" Mick continued to put in coins while Ceri left him and tried to win a cuddly toy in the crane machine. It took him six goes, but eventually he got the small teddy bear. He gave it to Mick, who looked genuinely touched, and slightly embarrassed to receive it in public, especially when Ceri whispered in his ear. "It reminds me of you."

They got fish and chips and sat on a bench on the promenade. The sun dipped slowly down over the sea. They didn't talk for a while, just ate and stared at the waves as they flowed in and out over the sandy beach.

"This fish is good," Mick said finally. "Mum said you always got better fish and chips at the seaside. Which bit of Wales are you from?"

"Monmouth. It's a few miles over the border from Cheltenham. My parents are teachers. I've a sister and two brothers. Megan is my twin. My parents kept trying until they had a girl and got me as a bonus. My brothers, Ifan and Dylan, are older than us, and both are married with kids. We lived in a house provided by the school, which was sort of nice. My parents still live there. My sister is at university, training to be a doctor."

"Are you close? You know, being twins. They say twins are either close or hate each other."

Ceri nearly commented on Mick asking questions but held his tongue, not wanting to send him back into his shell. He figured Mick might share more of his past if he did the same.

"Megan and I are close. I miss her every day. She was the first person I told about being gay, or rather confirmed. She'd guessed a long time back. We talk online two or three times a week, but I don't see her as often now she's up in Leeds. She's the more grounded of the two of us. I should get up there more often. Perhaps we could go together sometime. Ifan, my oldest brother, is an electrician, and Dylan is a teacher. I *was* going to university…" He hesitated for a moment, not sure what to say next. He didn't want to explain about Dickhead. "But I also had dreams of being a professional skateboarder, winning competitions, so I got any job that paid money and practiced." He sighed.

"What is it?" Mick asked. "You still see your family, don't you?"

"Oh yeah, I wasn't told never to darken their door again or anything, even after they caught me in a compromising position with one of the other senior pupils." *Dickhead again.*

Mick's eyebrows rose at his confession.

"It's just I guess it's time I grew up and accepted I'm kidding myself I'll ever be good enough to win any prizes skateboarding. And I don't know whether to go to university. It's so expensive. I could end up thousands of pounds in debt."

"What would you study?" Mick asked, between mouthfuls of fish.

"Psychology. I've always been interested in behavior, from the time I realized I was different. I watched a program with people talking about what might have made them gay." He turned to face Mick. "This is a rather personal question, but I hope you trust me enough to answer — do you think of yourself as gay? You've only had sex with two people from what you told me. Have you ever fancied anyone else?"

Mick chewed his food slowly, giving him time, Ceri guessed, to think of an answer. "I was eighteen when I met Alfie. There was a girl called Sally at school, but she was only a friend. She stopped the others picking on me. I didn't have much to do with the boys. I didn't look at them, because I didn't want to be called names. I didn't attend regularly. Mum let me stay home when I wanted. I'd fill my time writing stories based on superheroes and science-fiction programs. My stories always had male heroes."

"Do you still write?" Ceri asked. "I'd love to read your work sometime."

Mick's whole body stiffened at the suggestion. "They're only scribbles. I doubt anyone else would want to read them."

"Don't put yourself down. You never know."

Mick shrugged, crumpled up the wrapping paper then threw the rubbish in the penguin-shaped bin next to the bench. "After Alfie died, I kept to myself. Wilf and Fred talked to me and Ruby tried to get me to go out, but no one else bothered with me until you came along. I'm twenty-four, though people always think I'm older. I've always chosen the path of least resistance. I nearly went back to Mum because I was scared to be on my own in the flat, but the flat and the things in it were my only connection to him, and I couldn't stand not to have his belongings around me. Sometimes, I still put out two plates for dinner."

"I've never lived in the same place for any time with the same person — not someone I was in a relationship with," Ceri said, matter-of-factly. "My longest boyfriend lasted a year. He and I got together in school."

"Was he the one they caught you with?"

Ceri nodded. "He was tall, dark, handsome and loaded. We traveled around during his gap year. I got seriously into skateboarding in Australia and improved quickly. I won a few prizes there. I was eighteen and a dreamer. After a year, we came back here. Richard's family had bought him a flat and car so he could be near them and get to university in Bristol. After a few months, he met someone else and dumped me. Now, I have a room in a house I share with four others. It's a bit of a pigsty, but it's cheap and means I can afford to run my bike." He shivered. The breeze had increased, and the sun had dipped over the horizon.

"We'd better get back," Ceri said. "Or I won't find my way in the dark."

Finally back at the hotel, after they'd lost their way a few times, Ceri opened two bottles of water from the machine and handed one to Mick, who sat watching the TV from the sofa bed. The large bed dominated the center of the room. Ceri sat on the chair and waited. He didn't want to press Mick into doing anything he didn't feel comfortable with. He knew the other man was unsure of himself and used to behaving in a certain way as far as sex was concerned. Ceri swallowed half the bottle of water then began to undo his boots.

"I've had a wonderful day," Mick said, in between swallows. "Can I sleep with you in the bed and see what happens? Would it be all right?"

"I'd like that," Ceri said, trying to remember the last time he'd slept the whole night with someone. He was simply looking forward to being in Mick's arms. Anything else would be a bonus.

By the time Ceri had finished in the bathroom, Mick was already in bed under the covers. Ceri flicked off the overhead lights, leaving just the lamplight and undressed quickly.

"Shall I turn off the lamp?" he asked.

"Please," Mick said. "I'm not ready to…"

"It's fine," Ceri replied. He turned off the remaining lamp and turned toward Mick. Now, the only light came in via the top of the curtains. Gradually, their eyes adjusted to the gloom.

Mick stretched out his arm and Ceri settled his head on his shoulder. Mick kissed his forehead ever so lightly while Ceri twirled his fingers through the hair on Mick's chest. It was softer than he'd expected, like he'd used good shampoo and conditioner on it. He found a nipple amongst the hair and squeezed it a little. Mick moaned.

"So d'you like that?" Ceri asked, moving his head so he could run his tongue around the hardened nub.

"Mmm," Mick replied, squirming a little.

Ceri continued the caress with his tongue. He ran his fingers over the other nipple at the same time. Mick writhed underneath his touch. Moving back up, Ceri kissed him and laughed. "Your beard tickles. Perhaps tomorrow we could style it." Mick groaned in reply, his mind obviously on other things.

"What d'you want to do?" Ceri asked. "I could blow you again."

"I don't know," Mick replied. "I'm not used being asked. With Alfie, I followed his lead, and we did what he wanted. He was so much more experienced than me, and he made me feel safe, loved, special. He liked me to…" He swallowed hard.

Ceri raised himself up onto one elbow. He could vaguely make out Mick's face in the darkness. He trailed his fingers absentmindedly up and down Mick's chest.

"It's okay. You don't have to tell me anything you don't want to, but it might help." *Did you ever get to choose what you did?* "Look, if it's easier, I'll tell you what

I like to do, okay? I've simple needs. I like to suck men off, and I like to be fucked. I prefer not to top. It's not my thing. Though, I suppose I could try." Ceri stared into space for a moment, considering his words. "Perhaps I should be more flexible, but I've always been a bottom, though my favorite position is on top. I'd love to ride you when you're ready."

Mick tensed beside him.

Bugger. Me and my big mouth. "I'm sorry, I've said too much, haven't I? I don't want to freak you out. It's all right, we'll just sleep. That's okay too. Being here with you, whatever we do, or don't do, is wonderful." *I'm babbling to fill the silence.* "Please say something, Mick."

"Close your eyes," Mick mumbled. "I need to say something, and I can't if you're looking at me."

"Okay, if it's easier." Ceri put his head on Mick's chest.

Mick took a breath and grabbed onto Ceri's hand. "I'm not used to talking about sex. I know there's porn out there, gay porn and things, but I haven't watched any."

A man who's never watched porn.

"Yeah, I know that's odd. I've no idea if what me and Alfie did was normal. Well, I know it wasn't normal. Normal is for men and women, not men who sleep with men."

Ceri let the comment pass.

"Meeting Alfie turned my entire world upside down. Suddenly I was someone. I was Alfie's boyfriend. I was part of a group, accepted, and every night I got to be at home with this incredibly attractive man. Alfie had a stressful job, and he worked long hours. He often had to deal with the injured and their relatives. Sometimes, when he'd had a successful shift, saved someone, he'd come home, and be so hyper. At other times, he'd be frustrated. Then, I let him do whatever he needed to do because it helped him." Mick stopped and took another breath.

Ceri squeezed his hand. "Go on. It's all right. I'm listening."

Mick took a long breath then let it go. "He liked me to be on my hands and knees, sometimes spread over the edge of the bed. Mostly he was careful and prepared me, but sometimes he pushed into me as soon as he could. I always knew when he needed to."

Ceri bit his lip, desperate to say something. Was Mick saying this bloke forced him? He didn't think so, but he felt uncomfortable listening. Sometimes, he welcomed a burn that edged into pain. He'd had sex without too much preparation—needs must when in a cubicle or up against a wall. Some of his encounters had been rough, and Dickhead had been none too careful at times, but Ceri always gave as good as he got, and he could wriggle out of difficult situations if things got tricky.

"I liked it—what we did," Mick continued. "He always took care of my needs too. He liked me to come while he was still inside me. After, he'd hold me in his arms, and we'd go to sleep."

Ceri had so many questions, so many thoughts running through his mind. He wanted to set Mick free, to let him choose for himself, but it wouldn't be easy. It sounded like Mick hadn't made any decisions in his life. Ceri loved to bottom, but it was his choice. He wanted to encourage Mick to help him find out what he liked, but Ceri didn't want to put him on the spot and ask him straight out.

"Ceri, are you…asleep?"

He squeezed Mick's hand. "No, I'm still listening."

"Will you teach me how to make you feel good? I knew what Alfie needed, but I've no idea how to behave around you. You say you want to be on top. I know what it means, but I've never had sex that way. I feel like I've such a lot to learn."

"Can I open my eyes now? I want you to kiss me," Ceri said.

"Yes, please."

Ceri looked up and waited for Mick to move towards him. He opened his mouth. Soft lips touched his own. Soft hair brushed across his chin. Mick tentatively pushed in his tongue, and Ceri sucked it slightly, adjusting his own as they tasted each other. Mick moved his hands up and down Ceri's back as he pushed closer. Aware of his own body's growing response, he ground his cock against Mick's thigh, creating a delicious friction. Ceri adjusted his position, so he was cock to cock with the other man. They rutted against each other, moaning and gasping for air. A familiar tingling sensation gathered at the base of Ceri's spine, and Mick tensed underneath him.

"Oh yeah, please, don't stop."

"I won't," Mick replied breathlessly. "I need..."

Ceri's orgasm came in waves as he pumped out warm, sticky liquid between them. Mick followed quickly, and they clung together in the dark, breathing heavily. A sheen of sweat covered their bodies, and the air filled with the smell of sex. It was intoxicating. Ceri laid his head on Mick's chest and idly wound the soft hair around his fingers, waiting for Mick to speak, desperate to know he had enjoyed the experience.

"That was amazing," Mick said, his breathing back under control. "But we need to move, or we'll end up stuck together."

Ceri raised his head and wriggled his groin once more. His heart did a little leap of joy at Mick's comment. "Yeah, it was. I know we should clean up, but I don't want to." He took a deep breath. "God, we smell good together. I want to keep it for now, and I'm tired. It must be all the fresh air. Tomorrow we'll buy some sex guide books, if we're brave enough. You like to read, don't you? I don't want to scare you, but I want to try all sorts of things with you."

"You're not scaring me," Mick whispered. "I love being with you." He ran his fingers through the sticky mess between them and licked each one in turn. Even so soon after, Ceri's cock twitched in response.

"We taste good," he said. "I want you to teach me all you know. I want to learn with you as well. Tomorrow, we can go to the convention, do some tourist things, dress up, have dinner, then see what happens. Now, I want you in my arms."

"Sounds good to me," Ceri agreed and snuggled down once more onto the soft hair of Mick's chest.

Chapter Six

Mick rubbed his swollen stomach. "I'm not sure this bike will move after all we've eaten this morning. It must be all this fresh air making me hungry." Mick grinned as he got on the bike behind Ceri. Somehow, breaking out of his usual routine was easier here, and fluffy eggs and crisp bacon tasted a lot more appetizing than Rice Krispies.

"I rarely eat a full breakfast," he continued. "I noticed you tucked into everything. I've no idea where you put it. Look at you, you're as thin as a rake. You must have hollow legs. I swear my stomach has grown several inches since we got up." He leaned forward before Ceri put his helmet on and whispered into his ear. "After the shower..."

Ceri looked over his shoulder. "Yeah, but you look so good now. Your beard is under control and it's way more sophisticated. You loved me doing it and don't you dare to deny it."

"Why would I?" Mick closed his eyes for a moment and felt the edge of the shaver over his skin once more.

The shower had developed into a bath they'd shared. Ceri had sat in front of him with clippers and shaver and turned his untidy beard into something neat and stylish. He had to admit it took years off him, even if he felt more exposed than he had for a while. Now Ceri was on about Mick getting his hair cut too. He'd said he wasn't sure, and Ceri had smiled and kissed him. He still didn't fully understand why Ceri had said, '*Good for you. Don't let me boss you around.*'

They spent the first hour roaming around the streets and arcades in Cardiff. In the end, neither of them had the guts to buy any of the books they found, although they were tempted by the gay *Kama Sutra*. Ceri had turned the pages while they stood and giggled at the illustrations until one of the shop assistants came and glared at them while they were using their hands and fingers to plan out the various positions.

"We can order it on the net," Ceri said as they fell out of the shop, still laughing. "I bet there's a DVD version. Just don't get it mixed up with your *Doctor Who* DVDs. Can you imagine what the cleaners would think if they heard such groaning coming from your office?" He clutched his crotch and moaned rather too loudly. People turned to look at them.

"Stop it," Mick said. "Come on, we need to get to the arena, or we'll miss the Doctors and companions talk. Then this afternoon we can do the bus tour. I want to see all the places they mentioned online."

The arena was already buzzing with people when they arrived. Mick spent the first few minutes staring at the cosplay from every show represented at the convention. "The theater we want is over there," he said, pointing. "Come on. We need to queue now to find a good seat. I can't believe we're going to see them in the flesh. Next time, we can get photos." Mick couldn't remember feeling this excited. Being with Ceri, being here, surrounded by like-minded people, was a dream come true. The hour passed quickly. After, they wandered around the stalls.

"Go on, treat yourself to a few T-shirts," Ceri said.

"I've never worn them, but I like yours." Ceri had chosen a T-shirt adorned with rainbow-colored Daleks shouting *exterminate*. "Should I? There's one with Captain Jack here." He held it against himself.

"Suits you," a stranger commented. "And who doesn't love Jack Harkness?"

After some deliberation, Mick bought three T-shirts and one for Ceri. "Now where?" he said. "We need to be at the castle by one-thirty. We could get a sandwich and drink. Don't want to eat too much or we'll spoil our dinner."

After parking the bike, they found a bench by the bus stop and sat watching the world go by. "It's a pity we don't have time to go in there," Mick said, pointing at the castle entrance. "Maybe next time." *Please let there be a next time.*

"There are so many places we could go," Ceri said. "Have bike, will travel."

A small crowd of people had arrived and stood waiting with a man holding up an umbrella, even though there was no sign of rain.

"We'd better get going," Mick said. He disliked lateness. Seeing a couple in front of them holding hands sent a surge of jealousy through him. He wanted to hold Ceri's hand to let everyone know this beautiful man was with him—really with him. Instead, they hurried over and gave their names to the guide who wore the blue suit and swishy coat of the Tenth Doctor.

"Right, everyone. Please try to keep up. We will stop at various points and I'll tell you a little of the history of this wonderful city of mine as well as its connections to *Doctor Who*."

The tour began on foot, visiting the store where Rose had worked, then the National Museum. The guide, whose name was Paul, described how the building had been used in various episodes, but especially one of Mick's favorite episodes about Vincent Van Gogh. Paul read the speech, and as they had Van Gogh's, tears stung Mick's eyes. He wiped his face, hoping no one had noticed.

Ceri nudged him. "Are you all right? It gets me too."

Mick nodded. "I'm glad we came, just for this."

The coach was waiting for them outside. The first spot they visited was the church the reapers had trapped Rose in when she'd rescued her father and changed time. Mick listened attentively to the guide, then looked around. Ceri whispered in his ear. "There are things I wished I'd done differently, but I suppose if nasty creatures appeared every time, then it might not be worth it."

"So many things," Mick agreed, then they were off again to the village they'd filmed as Leadworth.

Mick felt himself vibrate with excitement, like a kid in a shop about to be let loose on the huge jars of sweets when he stepped from the coach onto the green.

"Come on," Ceri said. "I know you're dying to tell me all about it."

Mick explained every scene. Others listened as well until Paul waved his umbrella to gather them together. He handed out scripts, and the group re-enacted a scene. Mick played Rory and was word perfect. He stood tall, not caring if people looked at him. Sometimes fiction made more sense to him than fact.

"You were brilliant," Ceri said when they'd finished him. "I'm so proud of you. I can just see you as Rory the Roman and I could be Amy Pond. I've the height and legs for her." He held one out. His skinny jeans showed every curve. "What d'you think?"

"Time to go again," Paul called, saving Mick's embarrassment at his red face. "Next stop, St. Fagan's Museum of Rural Life."

"We must come back here," Ceri said, as they looked around the grounds. "These old houses are amazing. I had no idea all this was here. There are so many places we could visit together, if you want to."

Mick smiled. *I don't think I've ever been this happy.*

Ceri grinned back at him.

"What?" he asked.

"You look different today," Ceri said. "You're even walking differently."

"Am I?" He immediately hunched over, letting his shoulders slump and glanced around.

"No, don't do that," Ceri said. "I like this Mick. I want to kiss this Mick." He grabbed Mick's hand and pulled him into another room within the small, cramped house. Mick couldn't help himself. He pressed Ceri against a wall and let his hands wander all over him.

"I know we shouldn't be doing this here, but I don't care," he said, as he plunged his tongue into Ceri's mouth.

"Nah," Ceri mumbled as he rutted against him.

"We're gonna get left behind," Mick continued before their open mouths reconnected in another bruising kiss. They battled with each other until Ceri gave in, letting Mick explore every inch of his teeth and mouth. Mick sucked on Ceri's bottom lip and he groaned in response.

"Need," Mick said. His cock hard now pressed against his briefs wanting out.

"What do you need?" Ceri said, in a low growl. "Tell me what you need from me. I'll give you anything you want."

"Want to fuck you," Mick replied. *Where the hell did that come from? Do I?* He pulled back to check Ceri's face.

"It would be my pleasure," Ceri said. "But perhaps here isn't the right place. Later, tonight I'm all yours."

Mick stopped. "Sorry, I don't know what... I don't usually... I mean I haven't." He blustered and spluttered.

"It's all right, Mick. Believe me, I don't mind. But you're right, we'd better get going. We don't want to get left behind." They ran toward the entrance laughing loudly and got on the coach.

On the way to the next place, there was a quiz. Mick knew the answer to every single question, and they won easily.

"Wow, you really are a fan, aren't you?" the woman in the seat in front of them said. Mick felt a familiar heat rush into his face.

"He is," Ceri replied for him. "I swear he loves the Doctor more than anyone else, even me."

Three hours had passed by the time the coach returned to Cardiff castle. Everyone thanked the guide and the driver. Mick and Ceri made their way back to the bike. Tonight, for the first time in many years, Mick would be eating out.

Mick had bought himself a black jacket to go over his black trousers, which he teamed with a white shirt and blue tie to go to the restaurant. Ceri wore black jeans and shirt with his leather jacket, and a lurid orange tie. He'd bought it because it matched his current hair color. Mick guessed they made an interesting couple when they walked into the restaurant. He looked around, his eyes darting everywhere.

"It's all right," Ceri said, touching his back. "I'm here. Choose what you want and if you're not sure — ask."

Mick thought he'd probably been in as many restaurants as Ceri, but making his own choices was new to him. The more he thought about it, the more he realized that his relationship with Alfie hadn't been what he'd thought it was. The news was full of examples of people caught in coercive and controlling situations. Mick had followed the wishes of his mother then Alfie. He'd taken so much for granted, but now with Ceri, everything was different.

They were seated straight away in a booth to one side, which gave a view of the kitchens. Mick checked out the menu.

"I know what I'm having," Ceri said. "Fungi ripieni, followed by arrabicata pasta. I love chili."

Mick read everything before deciding. "I'll have the calamari, followed by spaghetti carbonara. Can we share a garlic pizza with cheese, and a green salad? Also, I'm paying. You paid for the petrol, so that's only fair."

"I won't argue with you," Ceri replied. The waiter took their order and Mick glanced around the room. Typically, it was decorated with paintings of Italian places, photographs of anyone well known who'd been there and each table had a wine bottle containing a candle. It wasn't a massive room, but there were other sections above and below. Under the table, Ceri stroked his thigh, so Mick almost squeaked out loud when those fingers nearly reached his groin. He wasn't sure whether to laugh or be cross. They talked about their day, all they'd seen and Ceri's family, especially his sister. Mick asked questions. He didn't want to talk about his life either with Alfie or his mother.

"And they couldn't expel me with my parents working there and Richard being head boy. We were both old enough, and they knew I was gay. Dad tore ten strips off me yelling, though. Then there was the time me and Megan hung underwear from the flagpole for a bet."

"Sounds like you had fun," Mick replied.

"We did. My parents are good people, and Megan is the best sister anyone could hope for. She works bloody hard and she'll make a great doctor."

Throughout the night, Ceri flirted outrageously with him, touching his arm and telling him how handsome he looked. Mick blushed so many times he lost count.

"Please, I'm nothing special," he protested. "I'm short, overweight and hairy. I look like the bloke who played Sam in *Lord of the Rings*."

Ceri reached out his hand and touched Mick. "But Sam was the real hero of the book and film—always loyal, strong and incorruptible. Sam is my favorite character. And you're just the same and as hot as this pasta to me."

"Shush. Someone might hear you."

"I don't care." He leaned forward. "Tonight, I want you to have your wicked way with me, but first—desserts."

"Ceri, please," Mick said, heat rushing to his face again. "Not everyone needs to hear what you're saying. He glanced around, but no one appeared to have heard Ceri's words.

"Really?" Mick asked, leaning forward.

Ceri looked left then right, grinned, then moved closer to Mick. "Oh yeah, you've no idea how much I want to feel you inside me."

"Stop now, or I won't be able to get out from under this table if you continue to say such things."

Ceri whispered. "I love the thought of you all hard under there with your gorgeous cock desperate to take me to heaven and back. Shall we skip the desserts, then?"

The waitress standing behind them coughed, making them jump. Her smile wide, she used a hand to cover her mouth and suppress a giggle. "I assume you'd like the bill then, gentlemen. I'll fetch it now for you."

"She heard," Mick said.

"So what? Come on. Let's get the bill paid, find a taxi, get home then you can take all my clothes off, and do what you want with me."

By the time they got back to the hotel, Mick wasn't sure whether he could cope with the myriad feelings and emotions rushing through his head. Ceri wanted him. Ceri wanted Mick to fuck him, and Mick wanted it too, possibly more than he'd ever wanted anything in his life, but it scared the hell out of him as well. He wasn't used to feeling this way. He wanted Ceri under him with his arse in the air, waiting for him to take control. It thrilled and confused him in equal measure to find he could feel this way.

Throughout the taxi ride, Ceri stroked Mick's thigh, whispering in his ear about how much he wanted Mick to take him, describing all the positions they could use. In the end, he could stand no more.

"Stop, please," he begged in a whisper while checking the driver. Mick thought he'd come in his pants, right there in the taxi, just from listening to Ceri talk. Those slight Welsh vowels caught his imagination, and the way Ceri rolled some letters, almost growling out the word *arse*.

Mick had no memory of getting to the room. Ceri had grabbed his hand then pulled him along the corridor. Shaking, Mick fumbled with, then dropped, the key card. Ceri kissed his nose, retrieved the card, opened the door and entered first. Mick closed the door and threw his jacket over the chair. He hesitated for a few seconds, letting Ceri get to the bed first. Now, he stood there, welded to the spot, with the reality of Ceri in front of him.

"D'you want the lamps on?" Ceri asked. He was sitting casually, leaning back on his hands, waiting.

Surprising himself, Mick replied. "Yes, I want to see you."

Ceri flicked the switch. His shining eyes reflected the light.

Mick moved forward until he stood between Ceri's knees. Ceri untied Mick's tie, leaving it hanging around his neck. He ran his hands up Mick's chest underneath his shirt, pushing it up, then undid each button. His lips, teeth and tongue kissed, nibbled and licked Mick's stomach and chest. Those same hands then moved around, and Mick felt himself being pulled closer as fingers pressed into his arse cheeks hard enough to leave bruises. He leaned down and kissed Ceri's orange hair, then shrugged his open shirt from his shoulders. Ceri gazed up at him. Mick wasn't sure what he saw in those eyes. Lust, love—it didn't matter. There was certainly want and need, and his heart swelled in line with his cock, amazed a man as beautiful as Ceri wanted to make love with a man like him. He pulled at Ceri's orange tie.

"Take off your shirt," he demanded, sounding more confident than he truly felt. Ceri undid each button slowly and deliberately.

"Now the trousers."

Ceri toed off his shoes and undid his zip. He lifted his hips. "You take them off," he replied. "Take them off me and see how much I want you. My arse longs to be filled by you."

Mick hesitated again. Fear threatened to overwhelm him. *Come on, you can do this. He wants you to do this.*

"Please," Ceri continued. "I need you to look at me and want me."

Oh, do I want you? Mick took a firm hold and pulled the trousers down in one go. He gasped. "Flipping heck. You're not wearing any briefs." Ceri's cock sprang up, and Mick took in an excited breath. He sank to his knees and wrapped a hand around Ceri's erection then ran a thumb all the way from balls to tip, feeling each swollen vein until he wiped away the liquid seeping from the slit with one finger and sucked on it.

"Oh hell," Ceri groaned. "You're doing that on purpose, aren't you? Have you any idea how sexy you look?"

Mick shook his head and fell back on his heels. "I've never thought of myself as sexy."

Ceri grinned. "Well, I think you're awesomely sexy and I can't wait to be yours."

Heat rushed into Mick's face. He didn't want Ceri to see the tears at the corners of his eyes, so tipped forward, grasped the base of Ceri's cock and ran his tongue around the tip.

"You taste so good," he said, before enclosing the end in his mouth and sucking hard. Both men groaned as he probed under Ceri's foreskin. Mick then massaged Ceri's balls, one by one, letting them roll over his palm.

"Don't make me come yet," Ceri said. "I want to come with you inside me."

Mick lifted his gaze, stood and pulled down his pants, revealing his own erection. Ceri deliberately licked his lips then wrapped a hand around the base of Mick's cock and took the rest into his mouth as deep as he could. After a few up-and-down movements, he stopped, letting go with a popping sound. Mick placed one hand on Ceri's shoulder to steady himself.

"I can't wait to feel this inside me." He reached over to his toilet bag and pulled out condoms and lube. "Better to be safe," he said. "How d'you want me?"

"On your hands and knees," Mick replied. Mick hoped Ceri's shiver was one of anticipation, not fear, and halted for a moment as he positioned himself behind him on the bed. Ceri turned and smiled, giving Mick the reassurance he needed.

"Okay?" Ceri asked. "You know what to do, don't you? Or do you want me to prepare myself? I rarely need much, so don't worry if you want to get on with things."

"No, I want to open you up," Mick replied, unable to stop staring at the glorious sight in front of him

Mick got the supplies and put them next to him as he knelt behind Ceri. He touched Ceri's back, running both hands up to his shoulders then returning down his spine. He kissed each arse cheek and gently parted them until he could see his target. He leaned in and ran his tongue down the crack, wetting the entrance, but, not feeling confident enough to push his tongue inside, reached a hand around and gave Ceri's cock a stroke, then covered his fingers with the lube. He pressed one finger at the entrance and pushed easily past the ring of muscles. It was almost as if Ceri's arse was pulling him in.

"More," he breathed at Mick.

"Who's in charge?" Mick asked, surprised at his need to take control.

"You are," Ceri said. "But I warned you I'm a greedy bottom. I can also be a talker. I'm not exactly the strong and silent type in bed." Ceri groaned as Mick pushed in a second finger and searched for that little bump of gland. When he found it, he gently scissored his fingers.

"Oh, God," Ceri said. "I should have put a towel under me. I'm leaking all over the sheet."

Mick reached around. "So you are." He added a third finger without warning and was gratified to feel Ceri lurch underneath him. He leaned forward and whispered into his ear. "I'm going to fuck you now. I'm going to take my fingers out, put my cock into you and fuck you into this mattress. You are not to touch yourself, d'you hear? When you think you're close to coming, I want you to tell me and *I'll* touch *you*. D'you understand?" He could hardly believe he was saying all this, using these words, but Ceri had said he liked to talk.

"Yes, please," Ceri moaned. "Get your gorgeous cock inside me. I'm dying here."

Mick withdrew his fingers. It had been a while, but he managed the condom. He'd had lots of practice putting them on Alfie. He added more lube then lined his cock up with Ceri's arse. Slowly at first, still worried about getting it wrong, he pushed in, but there was little resistance and within seconds he was buried to the hilt. He had no words for how good or how right it felt to fuck Ceri. The sensation of tightness around his cock amazed him. For the first time in his life, he understood what it meant to be part of another person. Raw emotion threatened to overwhelm him. He blinked back the tears pricking his eyes.

"Move," Ceri said. "Please, I need you to move."

"Sorry, got lost for a moment. I can't believe I'm doing this." Mick pulled back then plunged back in, watching his cock disappear and reappear. It was incredible, so much heat. Just moving his body in and out and hearing Ceri whimper and moan below him. He didn't think he'd be able to hold on for long, not this first time.

"I'm close," he said. His balls tightened, and a tingle ran down his spine. His thighs slapped against Ceri's arse. He felt such power. Reaching around, he took Ceri's cock in one hand and began to pump it.

"Yes, harder," Ceri shouted. Then it was over. Ceri's arse contracted around him. Streams of warm liquid covered his hand, and he followed Ceri over the edge, pouring out years of frustration into the condom. He fell over Ceri's back as the other man collapsed below him.

"Bloody hell," he said, and he never swore, always fearing the slap of his mother's hand across the back of his head. The room smelled of sex and cum. He didn't want to pull out. He wanted to stay like this forever, never losing the connection the two of them had. He couldn't work out exactly how he felt, but tears streamed down his cheeks and over Ceri's back. He buried his head into the groove between Ceri's neck and shoulders, still breathing heavily.

Finally, he pulled out, taking care with the condom and putting it into the bin at the side of the bed before rolling away and staring down at the man he'd just made love with. Ceri turned onto his back, put his hands behind his head and grinned at him. Mick knelt on the bed and gazed back, trying to read what was going on behind those shining eyes. Ceri appeared pleased with himself. Yes, that was it. His skin glowed in the lamplight. Mick smiled back then straddled his thighs.

"Are you okay?" Ceri asked.

"Yes, I most certainly am. Was I all right for you? Did I get it right?" He couldn't hide the concern from his voice.

Ceri picked up his now flaccid cock. "Looking at this, I'd say you did. What about you? Did you enjoy it?"

Mick had to stop himself bouncing with excitement. He wanted to stick his head out of the window and shout out to the world to tell them what he'd done. He ran a hand up Ceri's chest, collecting cum on his fingers.

"I fell into the damp spot," Ceri said. He opened his mouth and licked each finger in turn. Mick couldn't believe it when his cock began to harden as Ceri sucked his thumb. He sat back up again, reluctantly.

"It was amazing," he replied, grinning like a Cheshire Cat. "I loved fucking you, and as soon as you'll let me, I want to do it again. And I want to keep doing it until we run out of positions and places to do it in, then I want to start all over again."

"Whoa, boy, give my arse enough time to recover!" Ceri said, laughing. "I've created a monster, or maybe just an addict. Not that I care. You can fuck me forever."

Mick stared at him. He knew the words he wanted to say, despite it being so soon, but he didn't know if he should say them. He guessed Ceri knew the words were there as well, hanging in the air, ready to be plucked if either of them was brave enough to reach out and take the risk. Ceri moved Mick's arm and slipped underneath it, resting his head on Mick's chest. Mick stared at the ceiling and the words remained unsaid. Tomorrow, they would return home, back to reality. Maybe Ceri had the same thought as him. Mick wanted to know what all this meant, but in the silence filling the room, neither of them found it within themselves to ask.

Chapter Seven

Mick sat on the back of Ceri's bike. He glanced around. "I wish we didn't have to leave here," he said.

Ceri glanced over his shoulder and smiled. "We can always come back if we want."

The words *if we're still together* remained unspoken. The end of their idyll had come far too quickly. They'd enjoyed a leisurely exploration of each other in the morning, followed by a large breakfast after building up quite an appetite. The return journey was quicker than the outward one as there was so much less traffic on Sundays, and Mick felt more comfortable holding on to Ceri. So much had changed in so little time, and it would take a while for him to get used to it.

Outside his building, Mick was reluctant to either leave Ceri, or invite him in. No one had been in the flat since Alfie had died. He wanted to have Ceri there with him. He wanted to cook for him. He loved cooking for others. He'd cooked for Alfie and his friends all the time, and Ceri looked like he could use more food. *Time to take another step into the unknown.*

"I'd better get off," Ceri said. "We both need to get some sleep before our shifts tonight. I'll see you in the morning, and we'll make some plans."

Mick swallowed his nervousness and spoke in a hesitant voice. "Would you like to come to dinner on Friday night if you're not working, or going out? I could make my spicy curry. I like it hot with lots of chilies."

"Me too. The hotter, the better." Ceri pressed into him and Mick glanced around to make sure no one could see them. He stepped back and Ceri almost fell forward until Mick put his arms out and caught him. Ceri peered up at him. Mick wrapped his arms around Ceri and pulled him in close, suddenly finding he didn't care if anyone saw them.

"I'd love to have dinner with you on Friday," Ceri said. "I can't remember the last time someone other than my mother made me a meal. I'll bring beer. I don't drink much so nothing too strong, but you can't have a hot curry without something cool to wash it down."

Ceri kissed Mick on the cheek. Grudgingly, Mick let him go and watched as he straddled his bike. He waved, then took the stairs two at a time. It had been a wonderful weekend.

* * * *

When Mick arrived at work that evening, Wilf was standing at the office door, waiting to go. He whistled when he saw Mick. "Loving the new look with the beard," he said. "How was your weekend?"

Mick made a valiant effort not to blush and murmured under his breath, "It was good. Cardiff is interesting."

"I hope skater boy treated you well." Wilf, being older, often treated Mick like someone who needed looking after. Mick nodded, keeping his face down as he rearranged the desk the way he liked it.

"Fair enough, I'll leave you to it then, lad."

Mick waited for Wilf to leave then finally sat down. In thirty minutes, he'd do his first round of the building. He checked the screens, opened his book and began to read.

The night passed more slowly than usual, perhaps because he checked the clock every ten minutes, hoping half an hour had passed, bringing Ceri's appearance nearer. The weekend's experiences filled his mind, distracting him from reading or streaming anything. As he'd walked around the building, he'd even found himself whistling a happy tune. Over the last few days, he'd done things he hadn't dreamed he'd ever do. Everything about the weekend had challenged him but being with Ceri had given him courage he hadn't known he had. He'd ridden a bike on a motorway. He'd stayed in a strange room and eaten out in a strange city with another man. But the most amazing thing was the sex — that had been mind-blowing. He could close his eyes and be there again, hearing Ceri telling him how good he made him feel.

He wished he had someone to talk to about all that had happened, not that he thought he could talk to anyone about the sex. Ceri made him feel possessive. He wanted the man all to himself and longed to bury himself in Ceri's sweet arse over and over again. He'd learned things about himself he hadn't known. He liked to top, to take control, and Ceri seemed to enjoy letting him whilst telling Mick what he wanted. Mick had felt on top of the world, and he wanted more.

At six-thirty, the buzzer sounded. Mick couldn't help but smile when he saw Ceri. He'd forgotten it was a new week, and so there might be a change in Ceri's hair color. It looked darker. Mick buzzed him in and watched as Ceri worked, filling up the machines and replacing the huge water bottles. Finally, he arrived at Mick's booth and leaned back against the table in front of him.

"You've dyed your hair," Mick said. "Purple suits you."

Ceri pulled Mick toward him. Placing his hands in the other man's hair, he thrust his groin closer to Mick's face.

"Is anyone around?" he asked.

"We can't," Mick said anxiously, looking at the screen which showed his office. Something inside him stirred when he saw he'd be able to watch himself take Ceri's cock into his mouth. Ceri had lit a spark which threatened to grow into an all-consuming fire. *What's happening to me? How am I even thinking these thoughts?* His cock had already responded to the proximity of Ceri's body to his own. Ceri turned to see where he was staring.

"Oh my God, I'll be able to watch us. Will there be a recording?" He reached for his fly and pulled down his zip. "I know you can swallow it all, so there'll be no mess."

Mick nervously checked all the monitors. There was no one anywhere near his office. He swallowed hard. *All I need to do is reach in and touch.* A hint of flesh revealed Ceri wasn't wearing any underwear. Mick longed to do as Ceri asked. He almost glanced at each shoulder to see if there was an angel on one and a devil on the other telling him to be good or bad. One glance up at Ceri's face and the angel had no chance.

Mick reached down and touched himself. The bulge made it clear what his body wanted him to do. He undid the top button of his trousers and reached for some tissues. He was going to do this. He was going to suck another man's cock in his place of work and watch himself doing it on camera. Fortunately, he knew how to delete the relevant part of the film. He glanced up at Ceri again. Seeing his eyes, almost black with lust, sent Mick over the edge. He plunged in and pulled out Ceri's now completely erect shaft. Ceri took in a deep breath and pulled Mick forward.

Mick relaxed his throat muscles and slid Ceri's cock all the way into his mouth, closed his lips and sucked hard before pulling back and doing it again.

"Oh, God, Mick. Your lips look so good around my cock." Each of them watched Mick move his mouth up and down the shaft. Ceri couldn't resist thrusting, and Mick let him take control and fuck his mouth.

"This is so hot," Ceri said as he reached down and massaged his balls. Mick knew he wasn't far from coming either and fisted his own cock harder.

"The things you do to me, Mick Flanagan. I can't last at all." Ceri groaned one last time. "Gonna come."

Mick swallowed every drop of the salty liquid, milking Ceri's cock to completion. Nothing escaped the confines of his lips. Mick followed soon after, pumping into his hand. He quickly cleaned up as Ceri tucked himself back into his jeans. The whole event was over in minutes. Ceri bent over and kissed Mick gently on his forehead.

"Are you sure you can't get us a copy?" he asked.

"I'll see what I can do. You're a bad influence on me, Ceri Llewellyn."

"I know. Good, isn't it?" He laughed, and Mick's heart melted.

"Too good. I've spent all night thinking about you. I've been half hard nearly all the time. I'll need to wear longer jackets for work. I'm not sure I can cope with this every time you visit."

Ceri put up his hands. "I promise I'll be good on Thursday as long as I get to ride you on Friday night. I can't wait to have you in me and under me. What time do you want me?"

Mick swallowed hard. The taste of Ceri still filled his mouth. He guessed his lips must be swollen too, and here he was, casually talking about riding him as if it was the most normal thing in the world for him to do. Mick couldn't help his reply. "All the time. But I'll expect you at seven, to eat."

Ceri leaned in and whispered, "Oh, I'll make sure I'm hungry. If I haven't had you until then, I'll be famished!" He brushed his hand over Mick's thigh, causing him to shiver.

"Go on, get out of here. I've got to sort this footage out. I can't imagine what Wilf would do if he saw it." It amazed Mick he didn't feel more embarrassed. "I'll see you Thursday morning then Friday night. Will you stay over?"

"Wild horses wouldn't drag me out of there. I intend to wear you out playing cowboys. I might even find a hat." Ceri chuckled, slapped his thigh and flounced out of the room. Mick pushed his chair back and watched him as he progressed to the rear door. There Ceri glanced over his shoulder and wiggled his arse. Mick couldn't wait until Friday, but first he had some film footage to deal with.

* * * *

Mick altered his routine and did an additional shop early Friday morning. He bought all the ingredients he needed for the curry. Even carrying out this simple task on a different day constituted a huge change in his life. He'd managed to erase the tape, but not save it. He hoped Ceri wouldn't be too disappointed. He couldn't believe he was standing there, frying chicken, regretting he hadn't been able to save a film of him sucking off his boyfriend, in his booth, whilst at work. *What!* His musings did an emergency stop.

So much of this statement should have made Mick pause, but the only word which caused him concern was "boyfriend." *Are we that? Are we boyfriends?* He stopped chopping.

I've only known him a few weeks.

But you like him.

He couldn't argue with that. *Probably more than like.* He glanced down. *Not now I'm making dinner.*

Mick took Ceri at his word and loaded the curry with spices and chili, making it eye-wateringly hot. He left the mixture to cook slowly for two hours, then cleaned the kitchen, making sure to put everything back in its place. He washed his hands, set the timer and returned to the living room.

With time on his hands, Mick opened his laptop and found the most recent entry in his story folder. He stared at the screen, reading the last few paragraphs, then began typing. It had been some time since he'd written anything, but his muse had returned and the words once again flowed out of him.

"So, Carlos, what trouble can you and your crew get into this time?" He sketched out the overall story of yet another adventure of Carlos and the Space Buccaneers, a haulage team who often flew too close to the sun with the cargo they carried. He'd written about this team and their adventures when he was young and alone, with only his imagination for company. Pages and pages of his scribbles, as Alfie had called them, remained boxed in the hall cupboard. They were practically all he had brought with him when he moved out of his childhood home into Alfie's flat — two boxes of scribbles and a few clothes Alfie had immediately decided needed burning, not wearing.

Two hours passed by more quickly than he thought possible while he wrote and wrote, producing a couple of thousand words, losing himself in rescuing his hero from yet another difficult situation. He loved creating new aliens for Carlos to face and defeat. The timer sounded. He padded to the kitchen and turned off the oven, then returned to his story for another couple of hours. The sound of the doorbell shook him out of this world and back into the real one.

He glanced at the clock. "Damn!" Where had the time gone? He stood then went to the door. Pressing the buzzer, he let Ceri in and waited for him to come up the stairs. At the door Ceri gave him a huge grin, kissed him and handed him a large, colorful bouquet.

"Flowers?" he asked. *Do men buy each other flowers?* He wasn't even sure there was a vase in the flat. Alfie didn't like them because they died then shed petals everywhere.

"These are lovely," he said. "You didn't need to. I'll find something to put them in. The living room is through there." His heart skipped a beat or two. For the first time in years there was someone else in the apartment.

Chapter Eight

Ceri gazed around the starkly painted main room with its rounded space formed from the tower at the corner of the three-story block. Here was a padded window seat perfect, in his view, for sitting and reading. "I hope the flowers go with the décor," he said, when Mick returned with the flowers and placed them on the wide windowsill.

"I brought a few beers as well." He handed over the bag. Puzzled, he wondered about Mick's book and DVD collection. He'd expected to see them wall to ceiling, but the walls had only black and white photographs of cityscapes in frames, and what must be a forty-two-inch plasma screen over the mantel.

"Any chance of one of those bottles?" he asked, conscious Mick hadn't spoken.

"Sorry, I should have offered you something. I'll get you a glass."

"The curry smells awesome and I'm starving." He threw his jacket over the back of the sofa.

"I need to reheat it and cook the rice," Mick explained, picking up the jacket. He returned from the kitchen with the beer in a glass and placed it on a coaster on the glass coffee table. He pointed at the white leather sofa. "Please, sit while I get everything organized."

Ceri hadn't seen such a sterile space in his life. It looked like something out of a magazine — one of those homes no one lived in. Instead of sitting, he walked over to the table and sat in front of the laptop. Curiosity got the better of him. After lifting the screen, he began to read. After reading a little of the current chapter, he scrolled back to the beginning and got lost in the story.

"What are you doing?" Mick yelled as he slammed down the screen, barely missing Ceri's fingers. "That's mine. I didn't say you could read it." Anger poured out of Mick. His other hand had balled into a fist.

Shocked, Ceri pushed back the chair. "I'm sorry, Mick. I didn't mean to, but I couldn't help myself. Did you write this?"

Mick snatched up the laptop and put it protectively under his arm. "Thought it was funny, did you?"

"In parts, but I thought I was supposed to laugh at those bits." Ceri put a hand on Mick's arm. "I love the story. I read the first chapter, then I couldn't stop myself reading more. It's good enough to be published. I want to know how it ends. Does Carlos escape the Bangaloos?"

Mick frowned at him. "There's no need to humor me. I know it's nothing special. I told you I've been writing stories about Carlos and his gang of Space Buccaneers for years — since I was a teenager. Anyway, it's nothing. Come on, the food's ready, so we'd better eat it while it's hot."

Ceri noted Mick took the laptop back into the kitchen with him.

Mick returned with two wonderfully aromatic bowls of curry and rice which he placed on the mats then handed Ceri the cutlery. Like the wall décor, the mats had black and white photographs and the cutlery checkered handles. He carefully lifted a spoonful of food, sniffed then tasted.

"Wow." The chili hit his tongue immediately. "This is awesome, and really hot. I like hot things, don't you?" Ceri put on what he thought was his sexiest voice, trying to lighten the mood, but Mick kept on eating. He'd been quiet since the laptop incident.

"Um," Ceri continued, studying the contents of the room. "I couldn't help but notice there aren't any books or DVDs on display. I expected you to have quite a collection."

Mick glanced up from his food. "I do. I keep them in boxes in the hall cupboard. Alfie didn't like clutter. He said it disturbed the look of the room to have all those different colors on display."

"But…" Ceri began, then something made him stop. He finished his food quickly. "That was tasty, and exactly how I like it. Where's the bathroom? I need the loo." He wanted an excuse to have a nose around the place.

Mick pointed. "It's through that door and at the end of the little hallway."

Ceri knew there were two bedrooms. He opened the door opposite the main room. A clock and book sat on a small bedside unit. Next to them stood a photograph. He wanted to sneak inside and pick it up to have a closer look, but guessed it was Alfie. Everything here was white, just like in the living room, except for the blue duvet cover on the single bed. He closed the door then opened the door of the room farther down the small corridor. This room was much bigger with a king-sized bed. A uniform hung on the front of the wardrobe as if waiting for its owner and provided the only color in the otherwise white room. Ceri guessed Mick didn't sleep in here and hadn't since Alfie died. It wasn't quite a shrine, but it might as well have been.

He shut the door and found the bathroom, relieved himself then sat on the lid. He didn't know what to think. He knew Mick had his problems — the routines and such — but it didn't look as if he even lived in the apartment. Two toothbrushes still stood in a mug on the shelf above the sink. He got up and opened the cabinet. It contained shaving stuff, which obviously Mick wouldn't ever need, and aftershave, expensive aftershave which Mick would never use. There wasn't a thing out of place in this room either. Everything sparkled. He thought of his own shared bathroom where there were probably new life-forms attempting to evolve. Anger welled up inside him. Alfie might as well still be living there because Mick didn't, not really. He was like a ghost, without form or substance, who made no impact on his surroundings. It wasn't right. A knock at the door interrupted his train of thought.

"Are you all right? I haven't killed you, have I? You've been a while, I was worried."

"No, I'm fine. I'll be out now. Any chance of a coffee?"

"I bought ice cream for dessert first. I thought we might need it after the curry."

"Sounds good," Ceri replied, turning the tap on to wash his hands.

By the time he returned to the main room, Mick had put ice cream into bowls and was seated at the table waiting. His worried expression and furrowed brow suggested unease and Ceri wasn't sure what to say to him. He lifted the bowl. "Have you any sauce to go with this, like chocolate or caramel? Salted caramel is all the rage."

Mick frowned while pushing the ice cream around in the bowl. "No. Alfie didn't like sauce. He said it was messy."

Ceri reached over and stopped Mick's hand as it rose to his mouth. He said the next sentence as quietly and calmly as he could. "But I'm not Alfie, Mick, and he's not here anymore." Mick stared at him then rubbed his eyes. Ceri attempted to lighten the mood. He winked at Mick. "Lots of things you can do with chocolate sauce, not only put it on ice cream."

Without warning, Mick stood, sending his chair crashing to the floor. "I'd like you to leave. This isn't working out. I don't want you here. It's not right you being here."

"What?" Ceri asked. "I don't understand. You invited me. I thought you liked me." Mick glanced uneasily around the room anywhere except at Ceri. He held himself with his arms wrapped tightly around his body.

Ceri reached out a hand again, but Mick stepped back. Ceri searched for the right words to say. He didn't want to leave—not like this. "I know you have issues, Mick, and it doesn't matter to me. I like you, I like you a lot, but this isn't right, and you know it. This isn't your flat—it's his, and he's been dead three years. It should be full of your things. You're not even sleeping in the main bedroom, are you? You're like a lodger in your own home and — "

"Stop it!" Mick yelled, putting his hands to his ears. "Get out. I'm not listening to this." He grabbed Ceri's arm and pulled him toward the door. "I don't want to hurt you. Just go. Now. Please."

Ceri might have been thin, but he was wiry. He stood his ground. "If you throw me out and shut the door, you may as well be burying yourself in your own coffin. He's the one who's dead, Mick, not you. You weren't dead in that hotel room when you came, shouting my name, with your cock buried deep inside me. I bet you'd never felt more alive."

Mick tugged at his arm once more.

"All right, I'll go, but don't think this is it. I won't give up easily. I'll fight for you, Mick. I'll even fight a dead man if I have to." He opened the door and stepped out. Without another word, Mick slammed it behind him. Even through the wood, Ceri could hear him crying. He had no idea what to do.

* * * *

Ceri spent the weekend at the skate park. He needed to take his mind off what had happened Friday night. He hadn't slept much since then, so he figured if he wore himself out, he might manage a few hours before he went back to work on Sunday night. By Sunday afternoon, his body ached, and he'd made mistake after mistake. He picked up his board then sat and watched the others making move after move.

Enough. He resisted the temptation to dramatically throw his board to the ground and instead stared at the sky, hoping for inspiration. *I've no idea what to do. How do I fight a dead man? The dead make so few mistakes, and I've made so many.* He shook his head. *This time there will be no giving up.* For reasons Ceri couldn't fathom, Mick had got under his skin.

A Mick-shaped hole had left him empty in a way he'd not experienced before, not even when Dickhead had buggered off. No other area of comparison existed in his mind. Oh, he'd received a lot of pleasure from the sex and introducing Mick to new experiences, but seeing Mick smile brought him more joy than any fuck, something he hadn't experienced before. He wanted to protect Mick and be protected by him at the same time. *There's only one explanation. I'm in love for the first time in my life.* The thought sucker-punched him in the gut. But now it looked as if everything had gone wrong, unless somehow, he could work out a way of putting it right.

* * * *

Early Monday morning, Ceri pressed the buzzer at the office building with some trepidation. He had what he intended to say all planned out. Perhaps on neutral ground, Mick would listen to him. The buzzer sounded and he announced himself, but there was no answering voice, just the sound of a door unlocking. He completed his route around the building as quickly as he possible to give himself more time to talk, glancing up at the camera every so often to smile. He stopped outside the door of Mick's booth and ran his shaking hand through his still purple hair. He'd felt less nervous on the several occasions he'd stood outside his head teacher's office.

Taking nothing for granted, Ceri knocked three times on the woodwork. The voice which answered was not the one he expected. He eased open the door.

"Sorry, I thought Mick would be here."

Wilf occupied Mick's seat. Ceri couldn't help remembering what they'd done there only a week ago.

"He phoned in sick," Wilf replied "Said he'd eaten a dodgy curry. First time I've ever known him to be off work, so he must be bad. I'm surprised you didn't know what with you and him having dinner on Friday night."

Ceri didn't know how to reply. *I should have gone round there and not left him. What if he's...*

"When did he phone?" he asked. He intended to go straight round to Mick's flat after his shift.

"He phoned last night, so I stayed and did a double shift. He'd have done it for me. Is everything okay between you? You look kind of worried."

"We had a disagreement on Friday. I haven't spoken to him since. I was hoping he'd be here this morning."

Wilf nodded. "He's a good man, you know. I know he has his strange ways, but you get used to them. I'm sure you can sort things out."

"I don't know." Did Wilf know anything of Alfie, or even that Mick was gay?

Wilf put a hand on his arm. "Look, lad, if you're worried, I don't care about you and Mick being gay. My uncle was the same. My sister and I went to see him before he died. His partner was in bits, but he had no say over his treatment or anything else. My mum waltzed in and made all the decisions over a man she hadn't seen in twenty years, just because he preferred men. I thought it was wrong then, and I cheered loudly when they introduced same-sex marriage, so don't give me your *what the hell does he know* face, because I know, and I care. We look after Mick here and, looking at you, I guess something serious has happened."

Ceri nodded. "We had a row about his dead boyfriend, and I don't know what to do about it."

"Ah, the wonderful Alfie. Mick has talked about him occasionally. I always thought there was something a bit off about him. You need to get Mick out of the flat. I went there once. He wouldn't even let me in—said Alfie wouldn't have wanted strangers there. He'd been dead for two years then. I thought with him inviting you, he might have…moved on. Do me a favor, will you? Get around there and at least check he's okay."

"I was planning to. Even if he won't let me in, I'll see if he's all right."

"Good lad. This is my number. Text me and let me know please, or I won't get any sleep today."

Ceri took the piece of paper. "Thanks," he mumbled. "And thanks for the other stuff as well. Mick's a special person."

"That he is, lad."

Fifteen minutes later, Ceri stood at the side of his van, watching the windows of Mick's apartment. The main room light was on and a shadow moved behind the curtains. At least Mick hadn't done anything stupid. Ceri longed to go up and talk to him, but his feet remained rooted to the spot. His phone rang. He'd told his boss he was running late, but he knew he'd have to go soon. He needed someone to listen to him, so he'd talk to the one person he'd always relied on to tell him the truth—his sister, Megan.

Chapter Nine

Since he had a few days' holiday owing, Ceri checked with his boss and took the time off. He needed to work out what to do. He wouldn't give up on Mick, but he also knew he couldn't burst in all guns blazing and demand the other man give up his dead love, either. He also looked forward to being in the same room as Megan, rather than seeing her through a screen. He'd mentioned he was seeing someone during their regular calls, but, despite Megan's probing, he hadn't given any details as it was early days. Time had passed quickly, and it had been months since he'd last visited Leeds. Now in her third year of medical school and on one of her rotations, Megan was currently at a general practice, shadowing the doctors.

Ceri worked until Wednesday morning, got a few hours' sleep then set off to Yorkshire. Megan lived with her best friend, Sophie, who she'd known since they met over a Petri dish in her first year of medical school. They'd shared accommodation ever since.

After a thankfully straightforward journey, Ceri finally arrived at their house. He still found these back-to-back buildings confusing — all these houses jammed together with no back entrances and no gardens. Even though many of the streets been condemned since the nineteen-seventies, only some had been demolished and others, like this one, had been bought by private landlords who'd updated and improved them as residences for students. Ceri chained his bike to a couple of drainpipes and hoped it would stay safe.

Sophie greeted him at the door and smiled. "You got here okay, then. Loving the hair color. It suits you. Come in. Megan's running late. The GP surgery she's at has extended hours today, so she's still there, and you never know how long it will take if something happens. Are you hungry?"

"No, I'm fine. I got a sandwich on the way up. Can I dump this bag somewhere?"

"Sure, put it at the side of the sofa. We'll sort stuff out later. You'll have a coffee though, won't you? I need one to keep myself awake, then I've got to hit the books again. Final exams aren't far away now."

"Yeah, coffee would be good." Ceri sat on the sofa and watched Sophie go into the kitchen, the only other room downstairs. One bedroom and a bathroom occupied the first floor, and above, the loft had been converted into another bedroom. These houses were small but plenty big enough for the two, and at least the fittings were modern. Students demanded much more for their money these days.

Sophie was tall, at nearly six feet, with short red hair and striking green eyes, and Ceri had always thought would make a great model, but he'd never seen her dressed in anything but a shirt and jeans, and although he told himself off for stereotyping, he'd often wondered about her.

"There you go." Sophie handed him the coffee. He glanced around at the bright and comfortable room and had to admit these student digs were way better than the one room he had in a shared house.

"So," Sophie said, sitting in the chair opposite him. "Megs says your love life is a bit of a mess." It was a statement, not a question.

Ceri sighed. "Yes, I suppose you could say that. I should have guessed she'd tell you, but d'you mind if we wait until Megs gets here so I don't have to say things twice?" He yawned and stretched his arms. Maybe he needed a snooze after all, and even the coffee wasn't stopping his eyelids from edging downwards.

Sophie uncrossed her legs and leaned toward him. "You look done in. Why don't you grab a couple of hours' sleep on the sofa? I've got work to do. By the time I've finished, hopefully Megs will be home and we'll have pasta and wine and talk love lives."

"Sounds like a plan," Ceri said, and in a few minutes, he was snoring quietly.

* * * *

When he woke up in the dark a few hours later, he wasn't sure where he was at first. A light peeped out from under the kitchen door and he heard and smelled cooking. His stomach rumbled in response. The front door burst open.

"You got here then," Megan said as she crossed the floor toward him and pulled him up into a hug. "It's so good to see you. Skinny as ever, I feel."

Sophie emerged from the kitchen. "Immaculate timing, as always. I've made the carbonara sauce, so I'll put the pasta on now and open the wine."

Megan collapsed on the sofa next to Ceri. "Please, after the day I've had, I need a drink." She handed over the carrier bag. "I got a couple more bottles just in case. We had a woman go into labor at the surgery. There was no time to get her to the hospital, so she ended up delivering there and then. I tell you, doing this job is enough to put you off most things for life. Still, they're both doing fine." She turned to face him. "So, little brother… You're in need of some advice. Well, I'm not sure you've come to the right place, but we'll do our best to help, won't we, Soph?"

Megan poured a glass for each of them. He knew it was a waste of time to refuse and, truth be told, he felt like getting blotto. "I might need a few of these," he said. Sophie disappeared back into the kitchen.

"So, how's your love life then, sis?" *Might as well get a question in first.* "The last one was Martin, wasn't it? He still on the scene?"

"He's about, but we're not joined at the hip."

"What about Sophie?" he whispered in her ear. "I always thought you and her…"

Megan punched his arm and glanced toward the kitchen. "You know we had one occasion together and nothing's changed since then. Anyway, I thought we were here to discuss you and this Mick bloke. I have to say, he doesn't sound like one of the usual bastards you choose to give you a hard time."

Sophie brought in the food, and they sat down with bowls in their laps.

"No, he isn't my usual sort. He's nice, but he's shy and geeky and has…issues."

"Issues?" Megan questioned. "What sort of issues?"

"Well, to start with, he has these routines, sort of like OCD, but not quite. More like coping mechanisms than a belief if you don't do things a certain way disaster will follow. Then there's his ex-boyfriend, and his mother. It's complicated, as they say. I don't know *all* the details."

"Is this ex still around then?" Megan asked, between mouthfuls.

"No, he's dead, and that's part of the problem. Mick's only been with this one bloke before me, who was older than him — a lot older, and more experienced. From what I can tell, this bloke controlled everything, and Mick's mum was much the same. Alfie, his ex, died suddenly there years ago — meningitis. Mick isn't good with people or making decisions." He twirled another forkful of pasta. "This food is great, Sophie."

"It sounds like you're taking on a lot here, Ceri. Are you sure this isn't your habit of collecting lame ducks rearing its ugly head? You know what you were like when we were young, always trying to make things better. You've simply moved from animals to people."

"Or is this you trying to find out what makes him tick?" Sophie asked.

"At first there was a bit of that, I'll admit. He's certainly nothing like my usual type. But there's something about him. He's different, and it makes him interesting, and a challenge. In some ways, he was almost as dead as his ex, and I've helped him to live, or at least I hope I have. He's like this hairy caterpillar, and boy, is he hairy. I want to see transform into a butterfly. God, this sounds clichéd, but he's got this inner beauty begging to be set free. I read a story he'd written the other day, and it was magical, like being taken to a whole new world, and it's going on in his head, but he doesn't think he's any good, or what he's written is any good. I want to make him believe."

Sophie and Megan looked at each other and smiled knowingly. He caught the look.

"All right, I know I've got it bad. I like him. We talk as well, you know. He's a big sci-fi fan, like me, and loves *Doctor Who*. I persuaded him to go to Cardiff with me to look around all the sites. We had such a good time. It was like he'd been let off the leash and could be himself."

"And the sex?" Sophie asked, swigging back another mouthful of wine.

Heat rushed into Ceri's face. He grinned. "The sex is amazing."

"So, what spoiled this paradise, because I'm getting somewhat envious hearing you describe him?" Megan said.

"I went to his flat. Alfie left him this gorgeous place, but there's nothing of Mick in it, even three years after Alfie died." He explained about the rooms and his conversation with Mick. "How do I get past his ghost? It was like Mick just existed there, making as little impact on his surroundings as possible." He put the bowl down on the table. "It's like he wants me, but it's hard for him. He's never been allowed to make his own decisions. He even buys those little packets of cereal and eats them in order. But he's so kind and gentle and yet has this inner core of strength. He makes me laugh and making him laugh intoxicates me."

"Bloody hell, Ceri, you *have* got it bad. You love this guy, don't you?" Megan said.

"I think I might. I want to show him things, life, you know? I want to set him free, but I must admit it scares me too. I haven't felt like this about anyone before."

"You know you might unleash a monster and not a butterfly," Megan said. "He might want to try more of the world."

"I guess I'm willing to take that chance. Any chance of another?" he asked, holding out his glass.

"Yes, I'll get another bottle. It's no wonder we're poor students," Megan replied. They talked further, catching up with all the family news. If Ceri had been expecting answers about Mick, he didn't get any.

"You have to decide for yourself, Ceri," Megan said. "At least you can see him on neutral ground at work. Perhaps he'll have had time to think too. Anyway, I'm knackered now. I need to get to bed, but I have swapped shifts with someone, so we can spend tomorrow and Saturday together. Tomorrow, we're going to shop and do lunch somewhere, then later, there's a late-night showing of *The Rocky Horror Show* at the Hyde Park. You know, the little old cinema we went to the last time you were here."

"Are we dressing up?" Ceri asked. "I have nothing with me. If you'd told me, I'd have brought the corset. I suppose I could dress a bit like Riff Raff."

"You've still got the corset?" Sophie asked.

"Oh yeah. I've yet to try that look with Mick, although I could try showing him the photos." He drifted off for a moment.

"We're going as Brad and Janet."

"I'm Brad," Sophie said. "Again."

* * * *

Over the next couple of days, Ceri relaxed and had fun. They talked a lot about Mick and what he should do. Instead of going into Leeds, they spent Saturday wandering around Knaresborough, and even got boats and went on the river. Sunday morning came around too soon.

"Thanks, sis, Sophie, it's been good. I'll try what you suggested and see what he says. You're right — it's time to admit how I feel, whatever happens."

Outside, Ceri hugged them both and put on his helmet. All he had to do was persuade Mick he was loved. That would work, wouldn't it?

Chapter Ten

Back at work, early Thursday morning, Mick was sitting on the edge of his seat, watching the CCTV feed from the loading bay. He needed to apologize to Ceri, but he wasn't sure how. His whole life had been turned upside down. His routine had always been safe and clear before meeting Ceri. The sound of the buzzer shook him from his thoughts, but the face staring at him wasn't the one he'd expected. He had a moment of panic before pressing the intercom button for the man to speak.

"Delivery," the stranger said.

"Where's Ceri, the usual person?" Mick asked nervously.

"On leave for a few days. I'm Martin. Can you get a move on? I'm on a schedule here." He held his identity badge up to the camera, and Mick let him in. He spent the next fifteen minutes trying to work out what Ceri's absence might mean. Mick glanced at a monitor. The delivery man had stopped. He was scratching his head as if puzzled about what to do next.

Mick tutted and pushed his chair back. "Flipping heck, he's lost." He dragged himself up and went to find the source of his problem.

"Fucking hell," the guy shouted as Mick came around the corner. "I wasn't expecting to see anyone up here."

Mick frowned. "I saw you'd gone the wrong way and thought I'd point you in the right direction."

"Thank goodness for that. Some of these buildings are like rabbit warrens. Lead on, then I can get out of your hair."

"I'm Mick." He didn't hold out his hand. He still found contact difficult. Martin didn't seem to notice and continued to talk as he followed Mick around.

"So d'you know Ceri?" Mick asked, in what he hoped was a casual tone.

"No, I just do the relief. He's back on Sunday night. I'm filling in until then."

Mick showed him where to go then returned to his desk. At least he knew Ceri was coming back, but what was he going to say to him? Mick had so many questions. Where had Ceri gone, and would he want anything to do with Mick when he came back? He needed to work out how he could put things right. Mick put his head in his hands. Over the last three years, he'd become used to being alone, but now, with the possibility he might have messed up this good thing he'd found, he felt more isolated than ever. *I am such an idiot.* Mick's head jerked up at a noise.

"You were miles away," Wilf said. "Time to change shift, lad. Not like you not to know. I see there's a new guy doing the round. Ceri told me yesterday he was off to see his sister in Leeds." Wilf stopped when he saw the look on Mick's face. He rested against the desk. "It upset him, not seeing you on Monday. He asked why you were off work, and he wasn't sure what to do. He's worried about you, Mick. I think he dropped by your place to make sure you were still alive. I guess you two had a fallout."

"Sort of. I had some thinking to do." Thinking was one word for it.

"Look, Mick, I can tell you're both unhappy. You know I don't care about you and him being gay. I told Ceri the same. You and I have known each other a while now, but recently you've been different. I know happiness when I see it, and since he's been around, you've smiled a lot more. Hell, Ruby even told me she'd heard you singing, and I guess that's all down to him and his rainbow hair. You and him have this connection, and it seems to me that there's not enough happiness in the world to not take the opportunity to grab some when it's on offer."

Mick remembered Wilf's wife was ill. He nodded. "I know but..."

Wilf held up his hands. "No buts. Don't let this chance to get a little for yourself pass you by. Grab it and hold it tight. Give him time, and he'll be back. Over the weekend, whatever's happened, ask yourself whether it matters more than him. Now, get off. It's supermarket day, isn't it?"

Mick nodded thoughtfully. "Thanks, Wilf, you're a good friend." He put a hand on Wilf's shoulder as he left—little things and baby steps.

He had to go home before he did his usual shop. He didn't need his ragged list these days, unless they changed the store around, but he didn't like to go to the supermarket without it. He found the list on the kitchen counter and put it in his pocket. The phone rang. Unlike many people, Mick still had his landline. After their argument, he'd ignored several rings in case it was Ceri, but now he knew Ceri was away, he picked up. As soon as he heard the irritating voice telling him his internet would be shut down, he pressed the red button ending the call. He pressed the green button to check for messages and heard a steady beep. Nervously, he followed the instructions and listened. At first, the message confused him. He'd expected to hear Ceri, but a female voice spoke his name.

"Mick, are you there? Pick up if you can hear this. It's Sally, Sally Heath. I know it's been a while, but I'm back in Cheltenham, and I wondered how you were. Call me, please." She gave a number. The next message said the same. He listened to the third message.

"Hi, Mick, it's Sally again. I thought I'd give you one more try. Mick, I don't know if you're even getting these messages. Alfie, if you're hearing this, I know you didn't like me, you made it clear enough, but I'd like to talk to Mick. Please give him my number."

Mick took a pen out of his pocket and wrote the number on the back of his shopping list. He sank back onto the sofa, wondering what to do. It had been so long since he'd talked to Sally. Alfie hadn't mentioned her back then. He rang the mobile phone number. Sally picked up after a few rings.

"Hello," she said sleepily.

"Sally? Sorry, I forgot how early it was."

"Mick, is that you? You got my message. I'm so glad you called. Don't worry, you didn't wake me. I'm off to the supermarket while it's quiet." Mick's heart leapt. It would be so good to talk to his old friend. She'd always taken care of him and never judged him.

"If it's the one on the retail park off Carter Street, they have a café there. I could meet you," he said. "I've got to do my shopping first, and I usually have breakfast after."

"Yes, that's the one I use. I can't wait to see you. I've so much to tell you. Oh, Mick, it's so good to hear your voice."

"You too," he said, though his stomach had done a few somersaults while they spoke. "I'll see you soon."

* * * *

It was quiet in the aisles, as it usually was this early in the morning. He thought he might meet Sally on the way around, but he bought his few things without seeing her. Finally, he made his way to the café and sat staring out through the window.

"Mick? That *is* you, isn't it, under the beard?"

He turned to see a shortish, blonde, heavily pregnant woman staring at him.

"Sally?" he questioned. "My goodness. You look so different." He stood, and she pulled him into a hug.

"Sorry I'm late. This little one was bouncing on my bladder again and I had to divert to the toilet before I even left the house. Then I got caught behind a tractor on a country road…"

He stared at her. "I can't believe it's you. Can I get you something? Sit down and take the weight off your feet."

"Tea would be good, and an egg and bacon sandwich. This little one gets so hungry."

He got them both tea and made the order, then sat back down.

She stared at him. "Wow, it's been so long since I've seen you. Last I knew, you'd moved in with Alfie. I went to London not long after, and ended up working in an estate agency, got married and now this one is due in less than a month. Phil, he's my husband, is on an early shift. He used to be in the Met police, he's a sergeant, but finally, after I'd badgered him so much, he got a transfer back here. I wanted to bring this little one up nearer home and out of the big city. Sorry, I'm talking too much as ever."

A waiter brought their rolls. Mick watched as Sally took a big bite.

"God, I've missed such salty goodness," she said, groaning.

Mick took a bite out of his bacon roll. "Do you know what you're having?" he asked between mouthfuls.

"No, we wanted it to be a surprise. I don't mind either way, and we've painted the nursery all colors of the rainbow, much to my mother's annoyance. We've got a house a little outside town. The garden is huge, which will give this one somewhere to play. But, enough of me — how are you? And how's Alfie?"

"He died, suddenly, three years ago."

She stopped chewing and swallowed, taking in his words. "Oh my God, I'm so sorry. Was it an accident?"

"No, meningitis. It only took a few hours."

"Oh my. I don't know what to say." She reached over and put her hand on his. He didn't pull away. At school, she'd been his protector and only friend.

"Is there anyone else now?"

He frowned.

She blushed. "Sorry, that was insensitive and crass. I still don't always think before I open my mouth."

"No, it's fine," he muttered. "There is someone, but...it's complicated." He wiped his eyes, then finished drinking his tea, not sure what to say.

Sally ate the last of her roll. "Complicated, eh? Sounds intriguing. Look, why don't you come to my house now? We can talk better there."

"What about my shopping?" Mick said, looking at the few bags around his feet.

"We can put it in my fridge. Phil insisted we get one of those big American things, so there'll be plenty of room. Come on, my car is outside. I can still fit in it."

Thirty minutes later, Mick found himself drinking more tea in Sally's large kitchen.

"Come on then, spill the beans. This man you've met. I'm assuming it's a man. What's happened?"

"His name is Ceri. I know, it's a strange name for a man, but he's Welsh. He's in his twenties, and he's nice to me."

"He sounds wonderful. Nice is good, isn't it? How did you meet him? You're not exactly the going-out kind."

"He works nights at my building, filling vending machines and water coolers. I'm a security guard there. He comes to our place twice a week. Ruby, one of the cleaners, told him about me, and he asked me out."

"Just like that?"

"Yeah, I know, not something I'm used to. I didn't say yes right away. You know me — too scared, but for some reason he persisted. He's...different. He dyes his hair every week, different colors, like the rainbow."

Sally laughed. "How oddly appropriate."

"He kept coming to talk to me and he was interesting. He didn't laugh at me like others have. He likes *Doctor Who* as well. We went to Cardiff together."

Her eyes opened wide. "What? Away? Together? Alone!" She frowned. "Sorry, none of my business and I've no right to judge, but knowing you, I wouldn't have expected you to be so impulsive."

Heat rushed to Mick's cheeks and the table suddenly became the most interesting thing in the room.

"I guess I've an answer to another question. Sounds like he likes you, and you like him, but I'm guessing there's a problem or two in paradise. You said it's complicated?"

Mick raised his head and nodded. "When Alfie died, he left me his flat. We'd lived together for three years…"

Sally interrupted before he could continue. "At least he did the right thing there. I tried ringing you a few times after you moved in with him. Alfie answered. He told me you were busy. You didn't ring me back, and you didn't have a mobile, so I gave up trying after I moved to London."

Mick frowned. "I didn't know you'd called. I always thought I'd annoyed you. Alfie told me you were probably jealous of us being happy together." He paused. "He lied to me, didn't he? I'm sorry. I didn't realize. I was so young then. I've learned so much recently about how he behaved towards me, thanks to Ceri and checking online. I didn't know back then how much he controlled me."

"I'm sorry too, Mick. I should have done more. I wasn't sure whether to tell you what he said the last time I called, when he told me to leave you alone. You were happy with him and had a new life. I should have tried harder. I should have warned you."

Mick shook his head. "I wouldn't have believed you back then. I *was* happy with Alfie. He took care of me. I felt safe and loved. And we had a good life, friends, and…but I don't know anymore. Was it all lies, Sally? Did he even love me?"

"I'm sure he did, in his own way, and you loved him."

"When he died, I was lost. I didn't have a clue what to do or how to live on my own. First there was Mum, then there was Alfie. I had to deal with bills and decisions. I couldn't do it, so I worked out a way to manage until Ceri came along. He says he wants to help me, to set me free, but he doesn't understand everything. It's been easier for me to have a routine and keep things the same all the time. This way, I don't have to make any new decisions, and I cope on my own."

He took a deep breath then another to fend off the feeling of panic, which threatened to overwhelm him. The shaking started. He meshed his fingers together to regain control and gulped in air, unable to stop. Tears had formed in the corner of his eyes. He looked down at his hands and tried to focus. His heart pounded so fast he thought it might jump out of his chest.

"It's okay. Take your time," Sally said to reassure him. "Breathe, short in and long out. It'll help." He took in air and tried to do as Sally said. Gradually, his breath slowed as the tension flowed out of his body. Sally took his hand.

"That's it. You're okay now. Breathe. I'll make us some more tea."

She busied herself with mugs and teabags while Mick managed to get his pulse back to normal.

"Sorry," he whispered. "I haven't had an attack for ages."

"We don't have to talk about Ceri or Alfie," Sally said, putting the mugs of tea on the table and taking a seat.

"No, I want to tell you." He took a deep breath. "I invited Ceri round to the flat for dinner. He was the first person to visit since Alfie died."

Sally jerked her head up. "What? In three years?"

"I thought it would be all right to have Ceri there, but he asked me awkward questions about my stuff, and why I didn't have it on display. He started saying things about Alfie, and I didn't know what to do, so I told him to leave."

"But was he right? Was Ceri right? Come on, Mick, no hiding from me. I know what life was like with your mother, not letting you do anything normal and controlling all you did. Is Alfie still calling the shots from beyond the grave?"

Mick couldn't help himself. His emotions overwhelming him, his body shook once more, but not with panic, more with regret. Tears rolled down his face uncontrollably. He rocked backward and forward until Sally's arms surrounded him, pulling him close.

"It's okay, Mick. It's okay. Let it all out. Let the grief out. You loved him, and he died, leaving you all alone. But you're not alone now. You have me and Ceri, and we'll help you, but you need to do something to help yourself break free from the past. You need to... Perhaps we should start with the flat."

"The flat?" he questioned, pulling himself out of her arms.

She held his hands. "Maybe we should remove his things, you know?"

"I'm not sure...I...can," Mick said, between breaths. Gradually, he returned to normal.

"Look," Sally continued. "Let's eat lunch, and I'll take you home and see what's what. We can talk about you, and Ceri, and getting him back. You love him, don't you?"

Mick nodded. "I think so. He makes me feel good about myself. He wants me to be myself, but the truth is, I'm not sure who I am. He read one of my stories and liked it."

Her smile warmed his heart. "You're still writing? I'm so glad. I always liked those tales you used to tell me at lunchtimes. As for the rest, let's eat then we'll begin, together, like we always used to. Deal?" She held up her palm, waiting for him.

He raised his hand to high-five, and grinned. "Deal."

Chapter Eleven

"It won't open itself, you know," Sally said, as he hesitated before putting the key into the lock. "Come on, Mick," she continued softly. "It'll be fine. We'll go through each room like we talked about. If you put it off, it'll get harder to go back in." She kept her voice calm, he noted. She'd always been the strong one in their relationship. At school, she'd talked him down more than once.

"All right." He pushed away the panic building in his chest. "Give me a minute. I know what you're saying is right." He pushed the key in fully and turned it but allowed Sally to go in first.

She took his hand, pulled him in and glanced around the hallway. "Let's start with the bedroom. Might as well take the bull by the horns and start with the worst."

Mick nodded but said nothing.

"Okay, where are the bin bags?" Now, there was a brisk tone to her voice. Mick wasn't unfamiliar with this one either.

"Under the sink in the kitchen." He didn't want to think about what he was doing. Mick knew she was right about starting before he changed his mind. He couldn't continue living this way, and he didn't want to. He led her through the living room to the inner hallway and the main bedroom. It had been a while since Mick had entered this room. He pushed the door open and sat at the end of the bed, staring at the green uniform hanging on the wardrobe door. He'd seen Alfie wearing it the first day they'd met. It all seemed so long ago now. He reached out and held the material between his fingers. He'd been happy with Alfie, hadn't he? He picked up the photograph of them both from beside the bed. "It wasn't *all* a lie, was it?"

"No, but it wasn't all the truth, either, Mick."

He jumped not expecting a reply — not realizing he'd said the words out loud.

"Okay. I got some bags. Are you still sure about taking his stuff to the charity shop?"

Mick nodded. "Someone may as well get the benefit of everything. I'm sure Alfie would approve. He was a paramedic after all, committed to helping others."

Sally took the uniform from the door, folded it and placed it on the bed. Inside the wardrobe, everything hung as it always had, neat, tidy and color coordinated.

"Right, let's take these off the hangers and fold them up." The brisk tone had returned.

Mick sat hugging himself, staring at the clothes until she touched his arm.

"I'll do this if you want me to, Mick. I know it's hard. I remember helping Mum when Grandma died."

He shook himself. "No, I need to do this. We'll put everything on the bed and fold it away into the bags."

They methodically took out the shirts then trousers from hangers and placed them in the black bags. Gradually, they worked through the whole wardrobe and the chest of drawers. Jumpers, T-shirts, socks, belts and ties were all placed in bags.

"What about this drawer?" Sally asked, pulling it open to reveal the contents before Mick could intervene. He groaned when she tried unsuccessfully to cover a grin with her hand. "He had some interesting underwear." She held one up. "Superman? Really?"

Mick smiled for the first time since they'd arrived.

"I guess these mean something to you, right?" Sally asked.

"Yeah, he wore them the first night we slept together. I laughed so much, he got into a bit of a huff until he laughed too. He was good to me the first night, and careful. It was my first time...with anyone."

Sally glanced at him for a moment as he struggled to blink back his tears.

"Sorry, I'm being ridiculous. All I seem to do is cry."

She reached over and gently touched his shoulder. The warmth comforted him. "You could keep them," Sally continued. "You know, as a reminder of the good times."

"Isn't keeping them a bit odd?" Mick asked. "A pair of underpants, I mean."

Sally stared at him. "You can keep what you bloody well want to keep. There's only me and you here. Perhaps you should have a box with a few keepsakes, photos, etcetera, and well, pants. Whatever works for you. There's no wrong thing." She closed the last drawer. "Is that everything of his in here?"

"There's just the uniform. Perhaps I should return it to the ambulance people. I don't want it."

"Sure?"

"Yeah, I'll keep the cufflinks and a few other things. I'll get a box to put them in. I don't want to get rid of him completely. I loved him."

"Will you move back in?" Sally asked quietly.

Mick glanced around the room. "I don't think I want to. I don't want to be here at all now. There are too many memories. It's time to move on."

Sally bounced down next to him on the bed. "Then why don't you sell up? Remember, I'm a professional. This place would sell like hot cakes."

"But where would I go? Even if Ceri wants me back, he lives in one room. This is all I know, and I'm not going back to my mother."

"Have you seen her recently?"

"I haven't seen her since the day I went off with Alfie. She told me if I left, I was dead to her. She said she didn't want a faggot for a son."

Sally flinched at his words and blinked back her tears. She put one hand protectively on her stomach. "I can't imagine ever not loving my child, no matter what they did, or who they chose to be with. Why don't you come and stay with Phil and me? We've got a spare bedroom. I'll help you sell this place, then you can decide what you want to do. You'll have choices."

Mick couldn't believe what she was offering. "But you're about to give birth. I'll get in the way. And what about Phil? He won't want some odd-looking bloke with *issues* moving in with him."

Sally smiled. "Phil will do as he's told. Now, let's clear the bathroom then sort out some stuff for you to pack."

"I guess so," he said, unconvincingly.

She frowned and smacked the back of her hand. "Bloody hell. Now I'm doing it."

"What?" Mick asked.

"Telling you what to do." She turned to face him. "Look, Mick, you don't have to do anything you don't want to. You can stay here or come to ours. To be honest, I'd love your company. I haven't been the greatest at making friends here myself. My parents mean well but can be a bit overwhelming. Having you to stay would mean they can't descend and move in when the baby is born. My mum's been full of advice over everything, so you'd be helping me. And when this one is born, I'll need all the help I can get."

"You're *sure* Phil won't mind?"

"He'll be fine. I told him about you."

Mick sat open-mouthed in amazement. Why had Sally talked about him to her husband? "Okay, I'll stay with you. Thank you."

"Right. Practical issues. I guess this place is worth somewhere around a quarter of a million. Could be even more. You could do a lot with the money, Mick. It gives you some wiggle room whatever happens with Ceri. So, what do you want to do?"

Mick glanced around the room. "I need to pack some stuff today. I can come back for the other things another time. D'you really think I'll get a quarter of a million pounds for this place? Even saying that sounds mad."

"Somewhere near, I expect. It's a lovely Regency building, full of original features, and you have one of the tower rooms people love. It's a shame there's no balcony, but it's clean, and neutral. We'd better start loading the bags into the car. I'll wait there, and you can gather what you need. I thought you might like a bit of time on your own."

Mick nodded. Thirty minutes later, with everything stowed in the car, they were driving back to Sally's. "Have you decided what to do about Ceri yet?"

"I don't know if he'll want to see me anymore."

"But you want to see him?"

"Oh yes, I do. He's amazing. He lets me be me, and I've found I like me and he likes me. That sounded more complicated than I meant it to."

"It's okay, I get what you're saying, and Ceri will be back on Monday, won't he? You could bring him to ours, but I'd suggest somewhere neutral. I know! What about Pittsville Park? It has lakes to walk around and the Criss Cross café. You could suggest meeting there. They do a great breakfast."

Mick hesitated. "I'm not sure... No, you're right. I've got to start planning for myself. I'll ask him on Monday morning, if he's still interested."

Sally pulled the car into the parking space at the front of the house. Mick leaned over and kissed her cheek.

She laughed. "Hmm, tickles. Are you going to keep the beard?"

He stroked it. "For now. It's sort of become part of me, although Ceri shaped it and showed me how to use oil properly. It used to be all bushy like I was some sort of hipster."

"Can't see you following fashion. Come on, let's get in and order pizza with lots of pepperoni. This little one loves it hot even though it gives me chronic heartburn."

A little while later, Mick had unpacked his few things and was sitting with Sally on his new bed.

"I know this won't be easy," Sally said. "But now you'll have some time to be yourself."

"Trouble is, I'm not entirely sure who I am. I feel more like myself with Ceri, but I can't move in with him, not just like that, even if he wants me back. I haven't thought about anything much for the last three years, just lived each day."

"Perhaps you need to make a wish list. It might help you sort some things out."

Sitting in his bed later in the evening, he made his list. It was interesting. He could do so many of these things with Ceri, if they had a future together. It had only been a few days, but he missed him so much. Monday couldn't come soon enough.

* * * *

Ceri stood next to the entry door for some time while Mick watched him on the monitor. Eventually, he pressed the buzzer.

Mick took a breath and spoke. "Come on in. It's good to see you." He put his mug down, afraid his shaking hand might drop it.

"I'll do my round and then I'll pop into your office, if that's all right." Ceri sounded hesitant but didn't appear to be angry.

Relieved, Mick pressed the intercom again. He wanted to sound equally welcoming. "I'll be here in my office, waiting for you."

Mick gazed at the screen as Ceri moved around the building, picking up the large water bottles and putting them in place. Mick wasn't sure if he'd changed his hair color this time. It was hard to tell in black and white, but it looked like a different shade of gray. He tried to sing the nursery rhyme song to remember what was next. Should it be blue?

When his office door opened, Mick waited for Ceri to speak first.

"You're here then," Ceri said. A look of relief crossed his face, but Mick noted he didn't move any closer.

"I'm so glad. I worried when you weren't in last week." Ceri leaned against the door jamb, obviously not wanting to crowd him.

Mick smiled. "Did you think I'd swallow a bottle of pills or something?" He stopped smiling when he saw the serious expression on Ceri's face. *Idiot. How to say the wrong thing.* He wanted to get up and hug Ceri tightly, but he wasn't sure either of them was ready to return to the same level of intimacy yet.

Ceri stood up straight. "No, of course not. I don't know what I thought. Shit! I'm making a mess of this, aren't I? And I had everything planned."

"A bit, yes," Mick conceded. "But I shouldn't have said what I did. We need to talk, but not here. Wilf will be by in a few minutes so I can get out of here." He paused, wishing he could reach out and stroke Ceri's head. "I love the new color, and you've had it trimmed."

Ceri ran his fingers through his hair. "Yeah, Megan took off a couple of inches and colored it. I went for more of a mid-blue after the darker purple, even though it's supposed to be indigo." He paused. "Umm, when you say we need to talk, is that good or bad? Because often it's bad, and I…"

Mick put his hands up as Ceri babbled. "Good, I hope. You know Pittsville Park, the café, Criss Cross?"

"Yeah, I know it. The skate park isn't far from there. I still haven't taken you there yet to get you to have a go."

"No, you haven't, but I'm not sure I wouldn't break my neck. You could show me some of your moves though, if you wanted." *Did I mean that as innuendo?*

Ceri stared at him for a moment. Mick continued. "Meet me there in two hours at nine, and we'll have breakfast. A few things have happened since last week, and I've made a few decisions." He noted Ceri's puzzled expression. "Yeah, I know, me and decisions, but it's a strange new world I'm living in. Meet me at the café, and I'll explain things."

"All right, as you wish."

Mick grinned, knowing the quote.

"You know me. I love a bit of mysterious intrigue as much as the next person. I'll get off and see you later then. I haven't been to that cafe for ages. I might bring some bread to feed the ducks. There should be ducklings around at this time of year. We could go for a walk around the lake. It looks like it'll be sunny…if that's all right with you, of course. Sorry, I'm babbling again, aren't I? Okay, I'll see you later."

"I'm looking forward to it," Mick replied, adding a wink. He couldn't help smiling when Ceri nearly tripped over his own boots.

* * * *

A little while later, Ceri watched Mick walk toward where he was sitting outside the café. He'd parked the bike some distance away, but he could still see it from his chair. On the ride to the park, he'd tried to think of all the things he wanted to say, but in the end, he'd decided to wait and see what Mick had to tell him. He was conscious of not wanting to railroad or overcrowd him. All his life, Mick had done what other people wanted, and Ceri feared he could easily exert similar pressure. However much he wanted more from Mick, it couldn't be more than the man was prepared to give. So, no more plans — Ceri would simply listen. Mick took the seat opposite him.

"There's tea in the pot," Ceri said.

"Great, yes, I'd like some."

Ceri poured him a mug. "I haven't ordered yet. What d'you fancy?" he asked, handing Mick the menu. "I'm having a breakfast roll with bacon and egg."

"Sounds good," Mick agreed, after swallowing a few mouthfuls of tea. "I think I'll have the same. Stay there, I'll go."

Ceri drank his tea as he observed Mick disappear inside the shed-like building, grateful it was a reasonably warm day, although they provided lap blankets for cold weather. The tea was good — strong, as he liked it. He glanced around. The café was a timber building, painted in green to blend in with the surroundings. A few other people also sat outside, enjoying the early morning sunshine. To his left, the gardens stretched down to the upper lake. Perhaps they could walk down there later, unless Mick told him they were over, but he'd said it was good news, hadn't he? *Shit.* Now he was even babbling to himself and missed Mick's return.

"I didn't know if you wanted sauce, so I got some sachets of each. I guess there's still a lot we don't know about each other." Mick put the roll in front of Ceri and sat.

"Yes, I guess there is," Ceri agreed. "But we know what matters, don't we? Sorry, you said you'd made some decisions." He took a mouthful of roll. It tasted good. He licked at the egg yolk leaking down his chin until Mick reached over and dabbed it off with his napkin.

"I'm selling the flat."

Ceri shivered despite the warmth. "Oh, are you leaving Cheltenham?" His voice shook. "Where are you going?" He waited while Mick chewed the mouthful of roll he'd bitten off. Time appeared to stand still, and even the breeze seemed to be waiting before it blew through the trees once more.

"I'm not sure what I'm doing yet, but I can't stay there. I realized as much after you left. You were right. There's nothing of me in the flat. I guess I'd tried to hang on to Alfie, but Sally's helped me to look at things properly."

"Sally? Wasn't she your friend from school?"

"Yes, that's right. She's back in Cheltenham with her husband, and she called me last weekend. We met up. She's the same as she ever was, and we talked for ages. I'm staying with her now, and she also helped me sort out Alfie's stuff."

Ceri shook his head, unsure his ears had heard correctly. "Wow! A lot has happened. I didn't think you'd…" He stopped himself.

Mick placed a hand on his. "Do it? No, me neither, but Sally has helped me put things into perspective. I've also got an appointment to talk to a counselor about my problems. She had a cancellation so I can go next week. I've been reading about my behavior. I'm not sure what I have is OCD, but I have rituals like many people. I've discovered people have a variety of…coping mechanisms. Some issues can be linked to grief, and how you deal with the death of someone close to you. The thing is, even though I've been on my own for three years, I've never truly been by myself. I need to let go of the past and learn how to make choices for myself."

"But you're staying with Sally?" Ceri asked.

"For now, but I intend to rent somewhere, eventually. I'm staying there until the flat is sold and I decide where I want to be. There's nothing to keep me in Cheltenham. I could go anywhere. What's the phrase—the world is my oyster?"

"Oh, right, I see," Ceri murmured. He stared at the pattern on the table, unable to look Mick in the eye, afraid of what he might see, until Mick stretched out his hand and lifted Ceri's chin with his fingers.

Mick scrutinized his face. "There's no reason for you to stay here either, is there?"

Hope surged through Ceri's body and he sat up straight. "No, there isn't. Are you suggesting what I think you're suggesting? We haven't known each other for long, and you said we didn't know much about each other either and that you needed to be alone, so I thought you meant—"

Mick placed a finger on Ceri's lips. "I've lived on my own with Alfie's ghost for three years. I've shunned company. I've preferred living in my head with Carlos and his Space Buccaneers, but now I need something different. I'm hoping you need it too."

Ceri wondered what was coming next when Mick took a deep breath. His brown eyes seemed to gaze into the depths of Ceri's soul. He longed to reach out his tongue and taste him. Instead, this time *he* reached out and took Mick's hand in his own and waited for Mick to speak.

"I love you, Ceri. You've given me hope and shown me things about myself." He glanced around and lowered his voice. "And I don't only mean the sex, although that was fantastic. I'm hoping we get to have more."

"Really?" Ceri said, unable to keep the excitement out of his voice. "Because I was kinda hoping for more sex, too. In fact, I wish we could go off together right now." He stopped. He hadn't said it, and he needed to. He squeezed Mick's hand, not caring who saw. "I love you, too." Mick rewarded him with a huge grin and gleaming eyes.

"Good. But about the sex thing. It's a bit tricky. Sally's at home. She's only a few weeks away from giving birth to her first baby."

"Ah," Ceri said. "And I've only got one room with paper-thin walls. I'm definitely not taking you there. We could go to a hotel."

"I want to, Ceri, you know I do, but I need to get myself together. One thing I *have* decided is to send one of my stories off to a publisher to see what they say. I won't hold my breath, but at least I'm determined to try new things. We'll have our time together, and believe me, I'm looking forward to it more than anything."

Chapter Twelve

"Really? It's sold already?" Mick stared at the confirmation Sally showed him. It had only taken a week before two couples had put in offers for the flat, setting off a bidding war between them.

"Both couples loved it, so they both offered the full price. You could probably have pushed for even more." Sally passed him a coffee and sat opposite him at the kitchen table.

"I know, but each of them offered an extra ten thousand and the young couple bid first, so I wanted to play fair." Mick gazed at the email from the estate agent for a few moments then lifted his head and beamed at Sally with a grin all over his face.

"Oh. My. God. Over a quarter of a million pounds. I can't believe I'm saying those words out loud, and they want to move in quickly."

"You could put your stuff in storage then look around for somewhere to suit your needs. It depends on what you want to do now. I know you and Ceri have talked, so have you reached any decisions?" She sipped her tea, fidgeting in an effort to find a comfortable position. "Sorry, this baby kicks like a martial arts expert. Ceri?" she asked again.

Mick nodded. "Yeah, we've talked a bit about the future. We spent time walking around the lake and feeding the ducks. You were right to suggest meeting him there, and it was a lovely morning. It felt right being with him. It's always felt right from the beginning. Neither of us needs to stay in Cheltenham, and I don't think I want to, but I'm not sure where else to go. This town is all I've ever known. Other than going to Cardiff with Ceri, and a visit to the seaside when I was small, I haven't travelled in Britain. I *need* to know what Ceri wants."

Sally pulled a face.

"Yeah, I know it's my decision, but it's not that simple, is it? You and Phil had to sort things out before you moved back here. Ceri's in my life now, and I want him to stay there. I know he's considering university now he's worked out he's not skilled enough to be a professional skateboarder. I think visiting his sister confirmed a lot for him, and he's talked a bit about it. But he's got to apply and get accepted. His 'A' levels are good enough to get in, and I think he'd like to go to Leeds. He misses Megan. We were talking about it last night. Leeds is a busy place and I can write anywhere. And…"

"And what?" Sally asked.

"We've decided to date and get to know each other better. It'll help me get used to other people and to eating in public." The night before, they'd been to the cinema for their first date.

Ceri had dropped him off at work in the early evening after the film. They'd even kissed in front of

Ruby and Mary, who'd whistled at him as he went past. Warmth had spread through his insides as he watched Ceri leave.

Sally continued. "So, are you're waiting to see if he gets into Leeds? You know, having so much money will give you some choices. D'you think you're ready to move in together? You've only known him a few months, remember. Shit. I said I wasn't going to, but now I'm interfering and sounding like your mother again."

"Believe me, Sally, you sound nothing like my mother. For a start, you haven't used the word 'faggot' or 'queer', or told me I'll get AIDS, and anyway, how long does it take to know when it's right? I knew straightaway with Alfie."

Lines appeared between Sally's eyes as she pulled a face.

"I know, but Ceri's nothing like him. We can go anywhere, if my writing takes off, and even if it doesn't, the company does security all over the place, so I'm sure I could get something, but I'm not hurrying into a decision."

"Ow, ow," Sally cried out.

"What's the matter. Is it the baby?"

Sally shrugged. "It's probably nothing, they told me to expect a few twinges. I said this one kicks like a mule. I'll get us a salad together, all right?" She rose from the seat then clutched her stomach.

"Aarrgghh! Oh no. It's too soon." Liquid pooled around her feet. "Oh God, my waters have broken. First babies are supposed to be late, aren't they? Aarrgghh!" She doubled over.

Don't panic. You know what to do. All the same, he wished the baby had chosen a more convenient moment to want to come into the world. Mick helped her back onto a chair. "Somehow, I don't think this one knows they're not due yet. I'll call Phil, and an ambulance and get your bag. Don't worry. It'll be ages yet." Mick said, amazed at how calm he sounded.

The same could not be said of Sally. "Since when did you become a fucking expert? Ring. Now. Pleeaase! I'm not having this baby delivered by you on my kitchen floor."

* * * *

A few hours later, Mick had worn a groove in the floor of the waiting area pacing. Phil had arrived in time and immediately gone to join Sally on the ward. Mick had visited them briefly but decided to avoid the real business when the screaming began again — that would be taking friendship too far — but he didn't want to leave the hospital.

'It could be hours yet,' Sally had warned.

'It's all right. I'll stay until I have to go to work.' And so he'd sat outside and drunk far too much hot chocolate — nothing else from the vending machine was even near drinkable.

A nurse popped her head around the door. "D'you want to come in? Sally is asking for you."

Nervously, he entered the room. Sally was sitting up with the baby in her arms. Phil looked as tired as she did. "We have a daughter," Sally said.

Mick gazed at the screwed-up little face. "She's beautiful, just like her mother. Have you got a name yet?"

"Olivia." Sally yawned. "Sorry, I'm a bit tired, but I was lucky, I'm told. She came out in a hurry to meet the world."

"You did good, Sally." He shook Phil's hand. "I'll get off now and leave you both to it. I assume you'll be staying overnight."

"Not sure, but probably, then we'll be home sometime tomorrow, and the chaos will begin. Are you sure you still want to stay?"

"Of course. Is there anything you need me to do?" he asked them both.

"No, it's fine. Phil is taking some of his paternity leave. Let's hope she's not a screamer. And no, your next line isn't 'unlike her mother'. You haven't been at our place long enough to find out. Anyway, maybe I should be more worried about you and Ceri."

"Touché," Mick replied, grinning. "And there's my cue to leave. I'll see you tomorrow. Get some rest, both of you."

Once outside, he yawned. He'd had a few hours' sleep before lunch, but he obviously needed more. He called Ceri. "Hi, it's me."

"Hello, it's you. Everything okay?" Just the sound of Ceri's voice sent warmth surging through his chest.

"Yeah, everything's wonderful. I'm about to leave the hospital."

"What? Are you all right?"

"Don't worry, I'm fine. Sally went into labor early. She had a little girl who weighed in at six pound ten ounces. They've called her Olivia, and they're both doing well. Umm, something's happened, and we need to chat about it." He could almost feel Ceri tensing at the other end of the phone. "It's a good something, I promise, and will give us options, so don't panic. Can you pick me up at work tomorrow morning?"

"You're sure I don't need to worry? You promise?"

"I promise. I need to make more decisions, and I don't want to make them without you. You're important to me, Ceri."

He strolled down long hospital corridors as he talked. It was easy now, the conversation between them, and he could feel the spring in his step. His life had changed so much. He had a boyfriend, an old friend had returned and the money from the flat would give him choices which were his to make.

"I'll see you soon," he said happily. As he walked through A&E, he noticed a woman on a stretcher being rushed in by paramedics. He watched them for a moment whilst listening to Ceri talk. Memories of Alfie flooded through his mind. Doctors appeared from nowhere and crowded around the trolley. Slowly the features of the woman's face settled into a familiar pattern.

"Mum?" He vaguely heard Ceri say something but wasn't sure what. He stared again at the woman. She was older and thinner, and her hair was all but gone, but the woman lying on the trolley was most definitely his mother. It had been over six years since he'd seen or talked to her. He clicked off the phone and ran forward.

"That's my mum," he told the nearest nurse. "What's the matter with her?" The nurse stepped back as they pushed the trolley into a cubicle.

"I'm sorry, but you can't go in there. Let me find out what's happening, and I'll get back to you. Please take a seat while we treat your mother's injuries. She's unconscious." Tears flowed unbidden down his cheeks. "I can't tell you anything yet. All I know is that she had an accident at the hospice. I'll be with you as soon as I can."

The nurse disappeared only for a few minutes, but every moment of his life with his mother paraded across Mick's mind. He regretted what had happened, but his mother had made her choice. Now, she was ill and living in a hospice and she hadn't told him. Clearly, her hatred of him ran deep. He almost got up and left, but something kept him there.

"Mr. Flanagan?" He looked up to see the same nurse and nodded. "Would you come through to an interview room?" He sat down where she indicated, and she took the seat opposite him. "Do you have any identification we could look at? Your mother doesn't have any next of kin listed, and you can understand how we have to be careful."

Mick showed her his security badge from work. "Will this do? I am who I say I am, but I haven't seen my mother in six years. What's wrong with her?" He clasped his hands together to stop them shaking. Despite everything that had happened, she was still his mother. "I am her son, her only son. My name is Mick Flanagan. Her name is Marie Flanagan. She's forty-four years old. Her birthday is January twenty-eighth, nineteen seventy-five." She checked the information in her hand.

"That matches our records, Mr. Flanagan. Okay, your mother's had an accident. We think she fell over and hit her head, which rendered her unconscious. We need to do a few tests. She also has a suspected broken wrist."

"But you said she's in a hospice. You only go into one of those if you're dying, don't you? Tell me, please."

The nurse took his hand. "Your mother has breast cancer. She left it too long for treatment, so it's spread into her bones. She was lucky not to damage anything else in this fall. We'll treat her injuries, but it's only a matter of time. I'm sorry to be intrusive, but your mum has been here before and she hasn't mentioned you."

"We fell out six years ago when I moved in with my boyfriend. We'd always been close, but then I met Alfie. She said if I chose him, my boyfriend, then she didn't want to see me again. Alfie was a paramedic here."

"Oh my God, that Alfie. He died a few years back, didn't he? Meningitis, wasn't it? Really sudden."

"Yes, he died in a matter of hours. We were together for three years."

"And you haven't been back home since?" She paused. "Sorry, it's none of my business."

"It's okay, and no, I haven't been back. I'm still gay, that hasn't changed. I thought she still wouldn't want to see me. How long has she got?"

"We're not exactly sure. She moved into the hospice recently, and reluctantly. She's still unconscious, probably from the fall. We've given her some pain relief and put her on a monitor. We'll wait for her to come around then do some X-rays, but I'll take you in to see her if you still want to. Just wait here for me."

Jumbled thoughts and memories asserted themselves once more. He should be crying, remembering many of them. His phone buzzed again and this time he picked it up.

"Mick, what happened?" Ceri asked breathlessly.

"It's my mum. She's here, they brought her in as I was leaving. It was pure chance I saw her. She's dying, Ceri. She has terminal cancer. The nurse has gone to check if it's all right for me to sit in with her."

"D'you want me there too?" Ceri asked.

"Probably not a good idea. I'd better see her first. I'll let you know, okay? Can you phone work for me and let them know what's happened. I've no idea how long I'll be here."

"Don't worry. I'll sort out everything for you at this end. I love you."

"I love you too."

The nurse returned. "I'll take you to her."

He followed her down a corridor. She pulled back a curtain. Mick gazed down at the face of his mother for the first time in six years. She was basically skin and bone and had huge dark circles under her hollow eyes. He wanted to take her hand, but it looked so fragile he thought he would snap her bones. Her other arm was immobilized to protect it. He sat in the chair next to the bed.

"Are you going to admit her?"

"We're not sure. It depends on how she does and if she regains consciousness. She has a do not resuscitate order, so for now we wait."

* * * *

Over the next few hours, Mick sat next to the bed, attempting to remember the good times he'd had with his mother as well as the bad. He put his hand next to hers and leaned his head on the edge of the mattress. He yawned. It had been a long day. The clock told him it was now the early hours of the morning. Nursing staff came in and out, noting various details. The machine beeped steadily. After a little while, there was a twitch in the fingers next to him. He lifted his head and saw his mother's eyelids flicker. He pressed the button to call the nurse.

"Mum," he murmured, as she opened her eyes. "Mum, it's me, Mick. I'm here."

She stared at him through dull eyes. He wasn't sure what he'd expected.

The nurse came in. "Mrs. Flanagan, you lost consciousness when you had your fall and they brought you here. Your son is here too."

His mother frowned at the nurse. "Get him out. I'm ill enough without sharing his germs. God knows what he has by now."

"But, Mum, I'm fine. Please let me stay. You're…"

"Dying. Yes, I know." She coughed then spluttered. "Nurse."

The nurse gestured to the door. "You'd better wait outside, Mick. I'll talk to her."

Mick trudged into the corridor and fell onto the chair. All around him, people continued their lives. He couldn't handle this by himself. He switched on his phone and texted Ceri. *Please come now.*

Chapter Thirteen

After what seemed like hours, but in reality was only forty minutes, Ceri arrived in the waiting area of A&E, dressed in full black leathers and clutching his helmet. The outfit, combined with his blue hair, was striking enough to make people stare as he approached. Seeing Mick so desolate, Ceri didn't hesitate. He pulled Mick up into his arms and gave him a comforting hug. After a couple of minutes, Ceri let him go and took the seat next to him, keeping hold of his hand. A quick glance around the room revealed swiftly averted gazes. Thankfully Mick didn't seem concerned about the public display of affection.

"So, did I hear right?" Ceri asked. "Your mum is in here, and she's…" *How do I put this?* "Seriously ill? It's been, what, six years since you've seen her? I don't know what to say, Mick. Are you all right?" *Idiot. Of course he isn't.*

Mick shrugged. "I'm not sure how I feel. It was such a shock to see her lying there so pale and thin. The last time I saw her, she said I was tainted, that I'd always been tainted. I didn't understand what she meant back then. She'd always had this thing about people touching her. I thought she was afraid of their germs. She said if I was gay, I'd catch things from having sex with men—things that could kill me and her. She thought normal sex was dirty enough without such perversion."

He paused and wiped his eyes. Ceri squeezed his hand tighter, sending up a silent thanks for his own family who accepted him no matter how much he tried their patience.

"Well, you get the picture. She was pretty graphic."

"Shi…" Ceri stopped himself swearing, knowing Mick never did. "That's harsh." He hugged Mick again. "I was so lucky. Still, she is your mother, and you never know, she might have changed her mind about you. Perhaps things will be different when she regains consciousness."

Mick sighed. "She woke up a while back and threw me out of her cubicle. Six years has made no difference to her. I thought as she's dying, she might want to talk to me, but nothing's changed. Why does she have to be like this, Ceri? I'm her only child. For all my childhood, it was me and her against the world, and then nothing at all. I don't get it. I know she doesn't like men much, but mothers are supposed to love you no matter what, aren't they? Your parents didn't reject you."

"No, they didn't, but perhaps she thought it would always be you and her, and she didn't reckon on you having a relationship with anyone else. It was probably a bit of a shock to her." Ceri attempted to paint the best picture possible.

"She told me to choose, him or her. I loved them both. Alfie made me see how obsessed she was with me, and how it wasn't healthy. I thought she'd change when she saw I was happy, but she didn't, and now…" He took in a breath or two. "I should have tried to see her again after Alfie died, but I thought she'd try to pull me back into that life, and I couldn't face it, even if it meant being by myself. God, I'm such a mess. I've no idea why you put up with me, or why you want me."

"Fishing for compliments?" Ceri said, allowing himself a small chuckle. "I could give you a few reasons, but I don't think this is the venue for such a discussion, do you?"

Mick glanced around the crowded room. Ceri noted several heads went down to read papers, books or devices, as if they hadn't been listening to their conversation. A nurse approached them from the cubicle area and Ceri let go of Mick's hand.

"Any news?" Mick asked. The nurse glanced at Ceri. "It's okay. You can talk in front of Ceri. We're together." A surge of pleasure at Mick's words rushed through him and he pushed his arm through Mick's arm.

The nurse sighed. "I wish I had something more positive to tell you. She's confirmed you're her son, but she says she doesn't want to see you, not if you're still gay. I tried to reason with her. I'm sorry. I didn't think people like her existed anymore. It must have been tough for you having her as a mum and losing Alfie so suddenly." Mick nodded. "I explained Alfie had died a while back, and she seemed surprised, but she said as long as you were gay, well, she didn't use those exact words…"

"No, she wouldn't," Mick interjected.

The nurse took the seat next to him. "She just doesn't want to see you."

Mick nodded again. "I don't know what to do. She's so young. Why would she choose to die alone rather than have me with her? I don't understand. What will happen with her?"

"She'll probably return to the hospice tomorrow. We've taken X-rays and strapped up her arm. We need to keep her here for observation tonight in case she has a concussion. The hospice will make her as comfortable as possible when she returns. Perhaps you should try visiting her there. You never know, when she's given the situation some thought, she might give a little."

"You could do that," Ceri said hopefully.

Mick nodded "Perhaps. I suppose if she's had time to think, she might see me." He shifted in his seat. "It's probably best if we go now. I need to ring Phil and ask if there's anything I can do before Sally brings the baby home. Death and new life—it keeps going around, doesn't it?"

* * * *

Back in the car park, Ceri pulled out a spare jacket and helmet from the box on the back of his bike. "Back to Sally's then?" he asked. Mick shrugged and leaned into him. Ceri patted his back gently.

"I wonder what happened to Mum's stuff and the house. It's been in the family for years. Mum's lived there all her life. She was born there, and I think her mum was as well. I don't remember my grandmother— she died when I was small."

Intrigued, Ceri asked, "Where is it? We could swing by there now."

Mick gave him the address. It was slightly out of their way, but a little while later, they stood outside the boarded-up property. It was a large terraced house on three levels. It appeared rather run-down, and the paintwork needed attention, but an estate agent would say it had potential. There was a small gated front garden with overgrown rose bushes. They removed their helmets and sat on the low front wall.

"It looks so sad," Mick said. Ceri noted the weeds which now filled the spaces between the paving stones and bushes.

"She once caught Sally sitting here with me and shouted at her to get away. She used to call her *that girl*. *That* girl will get you into trouble. *That* girl will try to take you away. *That* girl is no better than she ought to be. *That* girl will lead you on and get pregnant, so you have to marry her." He shrugged. "She didn't know I was gay then."

"Did you always know you were interested in boys?" Ceri asked.

"I don't think I understood what it meant to be gay. I remember when Captain Jack Harkness first appeared on *Doctor Who*, she wasn't happy about me watching it then, but I loved Jack, and when he kissed the Doctor, it made me feel all gooey inside. I played my recording of it over and over. I soon worked out I was more interested in Jack and the Doctor than Rose, but I didn't add two and two — well, not really."

Ceri glanced around, but the pavements were devoid of people. "Did you ever, you know, touch yourself? My brother threatened to tie me in boxing gloves when he discovered I'd used all the toilet roll one night. We shared a bedroom, and he found bits stuffed under the bed."

"God. No. I thought Mum would know. She said only bad people did that — and filthy old men."

Ceri frowned, wanting to understand where her views came from. "Was she religious? Is that the origin of all this hatred?"

"No," Mick replied, shaking his head. "I think the family *were* originally Catholics, but she wasn't conventional. Anyway, religion would have interfered with her life. She kept us to ourselves and away from others as much as possible. She insisted I came home at lunchtime, and she allowed me to stay off school if I was even the slightest bit ill. The truant officer came around a lot. It must all sound so weird to you."

Ceri chuckled. "You're all right. I like weird."

"Oi, you two! Get off the wall. I'll call the police. That's private property." They turned to see an old man waving a stick at them from next door.

Mick stood. "It's all right, Mr. Brown, I'm Mick Flanagan. Remember. I used to live here with my mum until a few years back."

"Micky, is that you under that beard? Your mum's not here."

Ceri mouthed, "Micky," and grinned.

"I know, Mr. Brown. I saw her earlier."

"How's she doing? I didn't know where to find you, or if you even knew about her illness."

"She's not good, I'm afraid. Thanks for keeping an eye on the place for her. It's kind of you."

"This your young man then?" Mr. Brown asked.

"This is Ceri, and yes, he's my boyfriend."

Ceri held out his hand. "Good to meet you, Mr. Brown, sir," he said. He was pleasantly surprised when the old man shook his hand.

"I know your mum didn't hold with you lot. I tried to tell her over the fence that it took all sorts. I served with a few of you in the Navy. We all knew but turned a blind eye about what went on in the dark. They were as brave as any of us, braver some of them, so what did it matter? Not all were as enlightened as me though. She missed you, you know. When she did talk, which wasn't often, she'd talk about you when you were little. When you see her, say hello from me and tell her I've got our Jimmy looking after the garden at the back. She didn't want to leave her fruit and vegetables to go wild. I'll say this for your mother, she loved her garden. I'll get him to tidy up the front."

"Thank you. I'd appreciate that. I'll try to tell her," Mick said, his voice clearly shaking. He turned to Ceri. "We'd better get going. I need some sleep before work and so do you."

Ceri raised an eyebrow and waited until the old man had returned to his house. "D'you think Sally would mind if I crashed at yours rather than going home? I don't want to leave you on your own."

Mick breathed a long, what Ceri hoped was, a sigh of relief. He obviously didn't want to be on his own either. "That would be wonderful, and no, I'm sure Sally won't mind."

Forty minutes later, even squeezed together in Mick's bed, they both fell asleep seconds after their heads hit the pillow. Ceri woke up with a start when the door creaked opened, and Mick grabbed the sheet to cover them both. Sally stood staring in at them.

"Aww, look at you two lovebirds. And don't bother with the sheet, I've seen it all before, boys," Sally said laughing. "Although, I don't remember all the peach fuzz?"

Ceri ran his hand through Mick's chest hair. Mick didn't stop him but blushed bright red.

"You're home then," Mick said. "I hope you don't mind Ceri being here."

"No, of course not. You'll be the one complaining. We've discovered Olivia has a fine set of lungs. Phil's seeing if she settles, so I'd better help him, then I'll order some takeaway because I'm knackered and hungry. Do you want your usual?"

"Please," Mick said. "And add a meat feast for Ceri."

Sally chuckled as she left. "I might have guessed."

Chapter Fourteen

Mick phoned the hospice the next day to check if his mum was out of hospital. He explained a little of the situation.

"I'm sorry, but if she says she doesn't want to see you, we have to respect her wishes," the manager informed him. "I know how hard it must be, but our job is to make your mother's passing as painless and dignified as possible." She stopped for a moment as if she'd suddenly thought of something. "Hmm, look, we do have another patient here who doesn't get any visitors. He's a lovely man, in his nineties and still sharp as a pin. He has cancer as well and he's gay. His partner was a little older than him when he passed. Tommy told me they'd been together over sixty years. He loves to talk about old times, and he has some great stories. If you're here, perhaps your mum will relent. But, whatever, I know Tommy would love to have some handsome young men visit. It would raise his spirits no end."

Mick didn't hesitate. "I'd love to talk to him. I love stories myself. I'll bring Ceri, my partner." Wow, how he loved that description. "And then we can see what happens. I think it's a lovely idea." When he talked to Ceri, he was all for the visit, too. They went the next afternoon, before they were due at work.

The hospice turned out to be a bright and cheerful building with colorful pictures and murals on the walls. The manager, Marie Clifford, met them at reception and asked a helper to take them to Tommy's room.

"Hi, I'm Shelley." She was younger than Mick had expected. "I'll take you to see Tommy. He's excited to see you." They followed Shelley down the corridor.

"I didn't realize you could volunteer at these places," Mick said. "It must be difficult sometimes."

"It can be, but we try to make it a happy place. They were wonderful with my great-granddad. My mum's a volunteer too. We're having a jumble sale to raise funds next week, so if you've anything you'd like to donate, every pound helps. Ah, here we are." She knocked on the door then opened it. Tommy waited in his wheelchair. He was pale and hunched over, making him look so small. Mick noted oxygen under the chair. However, when Tommy lifted his head, his eyes twinkled with mischief.

"Ah, you must be the two lovely boys Mandy mentioned. Have you come to listen to an old man's stories then? Thank you for giving up your time."

"It's our pleasure. We've been looking forward to it. I'm Mick and this is Ceri. Do you want to stay here or...?"

"No, let's get out of this room. The grounds are lovely, and the weather is pleasant enough to sit on the patio. I like to get out there when I can. They're always busy here, so it's wonderful to have visitors. Tell me a little about yourselves while you push." His voice was light and shaky, but it was obvious he still had all his faculties. Mick told him about his mother as they walked.

"I can't understand it myself, but my parents were the same. Of course, attitudes were different back then. In my day, homosexuality was illegal. I'm glad I lived long enough to see things change. Malcolm and I got our civil partnership the day after they made it legal. He died a month later." He waved a frail hand. "No, don't feel sorry for me. We had a long life together, Malcolm and me. We met during the war."

"I've never met anyone who fought in the war for real," Ceri said. "We did World War Two in school."

"Well, I was there, lad, and I can tell you all sorts went on in those blackouts. There was more crime then too…none of this 'we're all in it together' stuff they like to spout. People took advantage of the dark for many nefarious activities. My Malcolm was older than me. He'd been in the reserves, so he joined up straight away and became a sergeant-major, training the new recruits. I knew from the moment I saw him in the parade ground, with his military bearing and carefully waxed mustache, that he was special. Silly, isn't it?" Mick glanced at Ceri. It hadn't been quite the same for them.

"He was standing to attention in full uniform, and he looked so smart, chest out, chin out, shoulders back, like the perfect example of a soldier from all the recruitment posters. I was a scrawny kid, all legs and arms. My uniform didn't fit properly. I remember him walking down the line, baton in hand, looking us up and down. I didn't know whether fear or excitement caused my shivering. In hindsight, I think it was quite a lot of both.

"He stopped in front of me and looked me up and down. *'Hmm, lad. We'll soon get some muscles on you.'* All I could think about were the muscles on *his* arms and chest, hidden under his uniform. He had that sandy-colored hair which occasionally strays into being ginger, and his mustache screamed military. I knew I was queer even then. I'd worked down the pit for a few years and the dark can hide a lot of things, but the moment I saw Malcolm, I knew he was the only man for me."

They reached the patio and Mick put the brakes on Tommy's chair before sitting on the bench next to him with Ceri opposite, listening as Tommy continued his story.

"Everybody knew what went on behind closed doors or in the dark. Some would have told on you, but most turned a blind eye if you did your job and didn't try it on with them. It was harder for us though, because Malcolm was in charge, but we managed. I couldn't believe my luck when he paid attention to me. We guessed they were training us for something special. None of us knew how long we'd have out there, totally exposed on the French sand. I was in the first wave on D-Day, at Sword Beach. It nearly killed Malcolm, watching me leave. He couldn't even wave, let alone hug me. A few of us shed one or two hidden tears in those trucks that day, I can tell you."

"Have you ever been back to France?" Ceri asked.

"Yes, we returned there a few times. It was strange the first time to see those wide beaches with children playing on them, instead of the landing craft and the blood-colored water. The Yanks got it worse at Omaha, of course. I'm sure you've seen the films, but we took casualties too. I was lucky. I only got hit in the shoulder, and that was the end of my war." Neither Ceri nor Mick said anything while Tommy stared into the distance.

"What did you and Malcolm do afterwards?" Ceri asked, after a little while. "It must have been difficult for you, given the legal situation at the time."

"After the war, I went back to digging coal down the pit in Clydach. My shoulder healed. Luckily it was my left. It was always weaker, but I could still swing a pickax. Malcolm stayed in the army for longer, but he came to dig alongside me. I put in a word for him, and he'd worked a coal face before in Yorkshire. Being down the pit was like being at war in some ways. You were in it together underground. We all needed each other, so no one said much. If you were one of them, and didn't flaunt it, you were okay."

Mick and Ceri spent nearly two hours listening to Tommy's stories of near escapes, of rock falls down the pit and how wonderful it felt to be legal after so many years.

"When Malcolm died in two thousand and five, we'd been together for over sixty years, and not many couples could say that. Oh, don't get me wrong—we weren't always perfect, but we knew the limits. I never loved anyone the way I loved him. Would you like to see a couple of photographs?"

"Please," Mick said.

Tommy reached into his jacket pocket and took out his wallet. He opened it up and passed it over. One showed two men in uniform and the other what Mick guessed was their wedding. He showed them to Ceri. "So many years," Tommy said, his voice shaking.

Ceri automatically grabbed Mick's hand and wiped away a tear. Tommy reached out somewhat and covered their hands with his own. "Don't let anyone tell you your love isn't real, isn't right, is against God's laws or any of the other poison some people spout, even today. Treasure it always and treasure each other. I'll try to speak to your mum, Mick. She can be a bit prickly, but she's been civil to me. I guess she hasn't worked out I'm a queer too. She has a thing about people touching her, from what I've seen, especially men, and only lets the female helpers come anywhere near. There's a story there, I guess."

Shelley appeared just as Tommy yawned. "Time for a rest now. You've had a busy afternoon."

"It's been our pleasure," Mick said, meaning it.

"And it's been lovely talking to you, too. Will you come again?"

"We'd love to," Ceri said. "It's people like you who helped people like us be able to live an open life. We know we've a lot to be grateful for."

* * * *

When they returned to Sally's, they still had a couple of hours to fill before work.

"Well, what shall we do with ourselves?" Ceri asked, grinning.

"Sally, Phil and the baby are visiting his mother until after dinner," Mick replied, grabbing Ceri's hand and pulling him toward the bedroom. If anyone had said he would be doing this only a few months ago, he wouldn't even have laughed, he'd simply have curled in on himself and died a little more inside. Yet here he was, laughing out loud and needing to be close to another person, wanting to be inside him more than anything else, longing for a connection. Somehow, he knew Ceri wanted the same. This was their tribute to all those men who had gone before them, risked imprisonment and campaigned for the freedom to be together.

Mick dragged Ceri into the bedroom, but then hesitated. He loved how Ceri had helped to create his new self, a man who understood his needs and wasn't afraid, but he didn't want to take anything for granted. Ceri plonked down on the bed and sat gazing up at him with his arms outstretched.

"Being with you makes me happier than I thought I could be. You're a good man, Mick Flanagan, but now I want you to be a very bad man."

Mick's heart and cock swelled at those words. "Oh, you do, do you? And how would I do that then?" he asked. With his confidence returned, he couldn't help smirking as he undid his belt. Ceri slipped off the divan and fell to his knees. Sometimes, Mick needed to pinch himself to make sure he wasn't dreaming. This gorgeous man followed his every move as he let his belt hang either side of the opening of his trousers. He lowered the zip slowly while Ceri licked his lips in anticipation. Slowly, Mick pulled out his cock and shook it in front of Ceri's beautiful mouth.

"Is this what you want?" Mick asked.

"You know it is." Ceri opened his lips eagerly, took the now erect shaft in his hands and guided it into his mouth. Mick groaned as soon as Ceri's tongue got going. He knew he shouldn't want to cry, watching Ceri move up and down, taking him all in then revealing him again, but his emotions kept jumping all over the place. He clutched Ceri's shoulders to steady himself.

Ceri kept his attention on Mick's cock, sucking and stroking. He ran the fingers of his free hand up Mick's chest. Mick had always felt self-conscious about his hairy body, but Ceri didn't seem to mind, judging by the way he was winding the auburn hair around his fingers. Mick moaned when Ceri tweaked his nipple.

"Feeling a bit on my own here," Mick managed between moans. The sensation of Ceri's soft mouth on his cock had become too much to bear, and he didn't want to come like this. He reluctantly pulled out then leaned down and kissed Ceri's upturned face. The longing he witnessed there shook him to his core. In those eyes, he saw love and desire, but above all, trust. That Ceri trusted him to decide was, for Mick, the most amazing part of this, and he loved it. He pulled Ceri up onto his feet then kissed Ceri's forehead, nose and mouth, gently at first then harder. He kicked off his trainers, trousers and briefs, and urged Ceri down onto the single bed.

"Too many clothes," Mick said, lying on top of Ceri. He buried his face in Ceri's neck and kissed him so hard it would leave a mark. Next, he reached between them and tugged at the button and zip holding up Ceri's jeans. He could feel him wriggling, trying to shrug off his clothes over his feet, which created a beautiful friction as their cocks rubbed together, lubricated by precum.

Ceri groaned and thrust his pelvis up to meet Mick's movements. "Feels so good," he said. "The things you do to me." Mick needed more skin on skin. He pulled his T-shirt off then pushed up Ceri's shirt, raising his arms above his head and holding them there for a minute, with the cotton fabric tied around them. He thrust upward again, trying to maintain the contact as their cocks slid against each other.

"Keep going," Ceri muttered. Mick still had one hand holding Ceri's arms above his head. The other, at his side, stopped him falling completely as he continued to move up and down. They established a rhythm, and Mick felt his orgasm gathering in his balls, like something alive and desperate to escape. He could think of any list he liked to prolong these sensations, but he couldn't stop this wave of feeling overwhelming his senses. Mick kissed Ceri hard, plunging his tongue into his mouth while Ceri thrust his cock up against him.

"With me," Mick whispered. "Come with me?" He screamed, "Now," and both men let themselves go, releasing hot liquid between their bodies until Mick rolled off and lay next to Ceri, idly running his fingers through the mess they'd made together. He put his fingers in Ceri's mouth and watched as he sucked them eagerly.

"Mmm," Ceri said, until Mick withdrew. He removed the shirt from his hands and reached down to wipe his own finger through the now cooling liquid. "Wow, we taste good." He placed his fingers in Mick's mouth. "Taste."

Mick twirled his tongue. His cock stirred immediately. Perhaps he could manage another round after all.

"We need to wash, or you'll end up a sticky mess. Will Sally's shower take both of us?" Ceri asked.

"If we stay close together," Mick said, smiling.

Ceri took his hand. "I love you," he said simply. "I know we've only known each other for a few months, but sometimes it's enough, isn't it?" He sat up. His words had left Mick too stunned to reply. *Ceri loves me.* His joy ended just as abruptly when he caught Ceri's serious expression. Panic rushed through him. *Is there a but?*

"What is it?" he asked. "Did I do something wrong?"

Ceri stroked his hair. "No. Stop worrying. It's just, well, I've decided to apply to Leeds. Seeing Megan again helped, but I don't want to leave you. Would you come with me, if you can?"

"Sounds like you're asking me to marry you," Mick said, without thinking.

"What would you say if I was?"

A thousand jumbled thoughts hit him all at once. *Marriage? Being married to Ceri. Being his husband.* "I've never even dreamed…" he whispered. "There's still a lot to discuss…"

Ceri's frown returned. "Sorry, I know. I don't know where the thought came from. It's okay. You don't have to answer. Ignore me. It's too soon."

Mick sat up and took Ceri's hand. "Shut up, you idiot. See this grin. Answering you is the easy bit. Ceri Llewellyn, I would love to marry you, but we need to deal with my mum and everything else first. Is that all right? I can't make any big decisions until then."

Ceri bounced on the mattress. "Of course it's all right. You do realize you've just accepted my proposal, don't you?"

"I suppose I have. Wow! I'm getting married." He pulled Ceri over on top of him and held him close, kissing every part of his face he could reach.

"Let's get into the shower now," Ceri said, winking at him. "I think I could go a second round." He leapt off the bed and ran out of the room. "Don't forget the supplies," he shouted happily. Mick took what he needed from the drawer and chased after him.

Chapter Fifteen

A few days passed before they could get back to see Tommy again. Every day, Mick rang the hospice to check on his mother. He knew it was only a matter of time before she died. It hurt thinking about her being there all alone. Her rejection had devastated him the first time. Naively, he'd imagined her coming to the flat to have dinner with him and Alfie, and how they would get on well because both loved him. And now he had Ceri, whereas she was all alone. Guilt consumed him even though it was her choice. More than anything, Mick wanted her to meet Ceri. He thought she'd at least want to die knowing her only son had found happiness. She was his mother and that should mean something, shouldn't it?

The roar of Ceri's bike outside the house caught his attention, so he grabbed his helmet from the rack in the hall. Ceri was taking his own helmet off when Mick opened the front door.

"Sorry, I didn't think. I didn't wake the baby, did I?"

"No, you're all right. They've taken her to the park as it's a sunny day. She's been brilliant most of the time and only screams when she's hungry or needs changing. She sleeps for hours. I don't think that's usual with babies, is it?"

"It depends," Ceri said. "Mum says I was a demanding baby, whereas Megan was well-behaved and could amuse herself. Fortunately, she could also amuse me. My brother's kids are the same, except for Jack, who is a nightmare according to my brother, Ifan. Have you ever thought about having kids?"

The question caught Mick unawares. "Me. No. I mean I'm gay, and well..." He paused, seeing Ceri's intense gaze.

"That doesn't matter nowadays," Ceri continued. "There are lots of ways. Look at all the gay celebrities who have kids. People adopt or use surrogates. There are so many possibilities."

From the tone of his voice and the questioning expression on his face, Mick could tell this mattered to Ceri. "I suppose so, but they're different to ordinary people like us. Do *you* want kids?"

Ceri shrugged. "Maybe... I haven't met anyone who I wanted to have kids with until now and, as we've talked about getting married, it's a possibility, isn't it?"

Mick bit his lip.

Ceri took hold of his hand. "Have I freaked you out? I have, haven't I? Sometimes I open my mouth without thinking. It's not a deal breaker. I love being an uncle."

Mick put his hands either side of Ceri's face and kissed him. "No, you haven't freaked me out. Things are moving a tad too fast for me perhaps, but it's good. It's like I've only been pretending to live for the last few years, and now I'm like some butterfly who's emerged out of a chrysalis, or should that be a moth, given I'm so hairy?"

Ceri smiled with obvious relief. "You're definitely a butterfly as far as I'm concerned, hair and all. Come on, we told Tommy we'd be there at two this afternoon and he said he had some news."

* * * *

Tommy sat waiting for them in the conservatory when they arrived. A woman was sitting playing cards with him. "I hope you won't be too warm in here, boys," he said. "The sun soothes these old arthritic bones of mine. Sit down. This is Emily. I took a chance and told her about the problem with your mum. I thought it might be easier if Emily talked to her, given her opinion of us queers."

Ceri flinched. It was odd how that word got to him while others embraced it. Tommy caught the movement. "Sorry, lad. I suppose it's not politically correct to use queer these days, but it's how we used to refer to each other. Times change, and so do the words you can and can't use. It's hard to keep up for an old man like me. And I've been called a lot worse than queer over the years."

"It's okay," Ceri said. "Some people use queer to describe themselves now, and you're right, being politically correct is a minefield. I suppose it depends how the word is used and by whom." He turned toward Emily. "I'm sorry, my mother would be asking where my manners are by now. It's a pleasure to meet you, Emily. This is Mick, and I'm Ceri. Mrs. Flanagan is Mick's mother."

Emily smiled at them then turned toward Mick and patted his hand. "Your mum's condition has declined, but I managed to have a chat with her yesterday. She's more confused now. She thought I was your grandmother, which meant she told me more than I expected. This won't be easy for you to hear, but I think it'll help you to understand her past."

Mick took a deep breath and clutched at Ceri's hand. "It'll be fine," Ceri assured him. "I'm here for you."

"I'm ready," Mick said.

Emily smiled. "You know your mum's family has lived in the same house for a few generations?" Mick nodded.

"That's what she always told me."

"Well, from what I could gather, it seems your great-grandmother lived there with her husband and your grandmother, until he ran off and left her for another man. They ran away to France because homosexuality wasn't illegal there. Your mum kept apologizing to me thinking I was Clara, your grandmother, for letting her down and producing a baby boy. I guess she'd been brought up to think men were not to be trusted and only useful for one thing, but she'd let some man have his way and ended up pregnant. She hoped you'd be a girl, but instead she gave birth to a boy, not the girl she wanted."

"And even worse I turned out to be gay like my great-grandfather."

"To put it bluntly — yes. She was crying and asking for forgiveness for failing her. I tried to tell her it was all right, but she got distressed, and I had to call for the nurse."

Mick's Adam's apple bobbed up and down as he swallowed hard, trying to hold back the tears. Ceri stroked his wrist, letting him know he was there and wasn't alone.

"That would explain something," Mick said. "When I started working for the security firm, I needed my birth certificate." Ceri felt him shaking.

"On my certificate, it stated I was a girl and my registered name was Michaela. I thought it had been a mistake, and I got it changed to Michael, which wasn't as easy as I thought. I had to show I hadn't had a sex-change operation and get confirmation from a doctor. Now, with what you've told me, I think Mum may have done it on purpose and lied to her mother about me being a girl because she was ashamed. She must have kept my hair long, to help convince her. Gran died before I was old enough to go to school. Mum would have had to tell the truth then. Perhaps she feels guilty for lying about me." He slumped next to Ceri and sighed. "I must have been such a disappointment to her."

Ceri put a hand on his arm. "She might also think she made you gay by treating you as a girl to begin with. Guilt is a powerful emotion, Mick. Seeing you now means she has to face all the mistakes she made, and all the lies, especially if she's getting confused now. It's not your fault. It's hers. She let *you* down. *You* did nothing wrong."

"That's easy to say, and deep down, I know it's true, but she's still my mum and, despite everything, I still love her and need to talk to her. I suppose I need some sort of closure, though I hate the word. We need to talk, no matter how painful it'll be for both of us."

None of them spoke for a little while, taking in what they'd heard. Another helper pushed a woman in a wheelchair to the corner on the other side of the conservatory and positioned her so she could look out of the windows at the gardens. It was a warm day, but the air conditioning was on, and the conservatory had roof blinds, so the room was a pleasant place for anyone who felt the cold, as many of the occupants of the hospice did. "I'll get you a cup of tea, Mrs. Flanagan."

Mick turned immediately.

"Oh hell," Ceri said, glancing in the same direction. Tommy stopped talking.

Mick leaned into Ceri and whispered into his ear. "What do we do? If she sees me, there could be a scene."

"You can both get out through the other doors if you're quick," Emily said, nudging Ceri. "We'll try to talk to her again, depending on how she is. She's probably dosed up with painkillers so won't notice much. They can make you a bit funny."

Mick glanced at Tommy. "It's all right, lad. I've got time left to me before I'm completely gaga, so you can come again and listen to my ramblings. You need to take stock and digest what you've heard today." He turned to Ceri. "And you look after him, you hear me?"

"I will," Ceri assured him. "And we'll be back. It was lovely to meet you, Emily."

Mick followed Ceri through the conservatory door and around the building, back to the car park. "Come on," Ceri said. He didn't want to go home yet. "Let's go for a ride and get out of town."

Mick nodded.

Ceri took them up Leckhampton Hill until he found a spot where he could park the bike and they could sit gazing over the panorama of fields and forests in front of them. He pulled Mick down on to the grass. "I'm sorry," Ceri said.

"What for?" Mick asked. "My crazy childhood had nothing to do with you. I don't remember much about the early stuff, just some images of long hair and dresses. I remember being given dolls to play with. Living with Mum was hard, but I didn't understand why. I always thought she didn't want me out of her sight because she loved me and wanted to protect me. She even tried to home school me for a while, but they wouldn't let her. I thought she worried about me being bullied, but instead, she was ashamed of me — ashamed she'd produced a boy rather than the girl she wanted. I've got everything wrong over the years, haven't I? Do you think she ever cared for me?" He brushed a tear from his cheek. "I feel like I've been nothing but a disappointment to her from the moment I was born."

Ceri put his arm around Mick's shoulder and held his head to his chest until the sobbing subsided. Red-hot anger burned inside him. How could any mother treat their son like she had treated Mick? He wanted to scream at her for what she'd done to her only child, what she was still doing. He held Mick until he was ready to talk once more, rocking him back and forth. It was a few minutes until they pulled apart.

Mick stared up at him with red eyes. Ceri put his hands either side of Mick's face. "I love you, Mick Flanagan, and I want to marry you. You are the nicest, kindest, and sexiest man I've ever met, and none of this is your fault. You're the victim here, and you need to understand that. And even if I have to keep telling you forever, I will. Do you understand what I'm saying to you? Until I met you, I kept kidding myself everything in my life was tickety-boo, but that world wasn't real. I was drifting, going from person to person trying to find…oh, I don't know, something, but now I have you and a plan for my future. I know what I want to do, and even better, I've got someone to think about other than me. I wouldn't change that for the world. No one has ever made me feel like you do, so don't you ever think you're worthless, because I need you in my life, even with your terrible beard and your need to eat everything in order of sell-by date. You aren't going back to the lonely life you had, because I won't let you, and I doubt Sally would either, not to mention we both need more Carlos and the Space Buccaneers."

Mick laughed. Ceri thought it was the most beautiful sound in the world. His heart skipped a beat as Mick peered up at him through auburn lashes, his brown eyes now sparkling again with hints of amber.

"I love you too. You've no idea how much. I thought my life was over before you came and shook me up. I still don't understand why you bothered, but I'm so glad you did. I'll talk to the counselor and hopefully he'll help."

Ceri put on a sad face, knowing he shouldn't but wishing Mick could confide in him.

Mick kissed his cheek. "Don't be hurt. I *will* talk to you eventually, but somehow, it's easier to talk to someone you don't know."

"It's all right. I know. I wasn't being serious."

"Good, because I've an appointment next week. In the meantime, we've got to sort out your application for university and find us somewhere to live. I can't change the past, Ceri, so I guess I'll have to learn to live with it, and if Mum won't talk to me again, I guess I'll just have to accept that too. As long as I have you, the world's all right." He leaned forward so their foreheads touched. Lost in their own little world, for a few minutes, nothing else mattered.

Chapter Sixteen

A few weeks passed. Mick talked to his counselor, confident she was helping him come to terms with everything. Once a week, he and Ceri visited Tommy in the hospice. Mick understood his mother's condition was deteriorating fast, but she still wouldn't see him.

"I've asked her again," the manager said. "I told her you wanted to talk to her, but she shook her head. I don't think you should give up, though, as this time she said *not yet,* so there may still be hope."

"That's good, isn't it?" Sally said later. "Maybe she *will* see you."

"Maybe. I just hope it isn't too late when she does." He picked up the parcel on the table and handed it to Sally. "It's for Olivia," he said. "I made them myself."

Sally opened the parcel and stared at the contents. "You made these?" she said, picking up the top matinee coat. "It's beautiful."

"I made them in different colors and there are booties and hats to match. I know they're old-fashioned—"

"I had no idea you could knit."

"He knits hats for premature babies," Ceri said.

Olivia grizzled in her basket. Sally picked her up and gently rocked her. "See what your Uncle Mick has made you. You'll be gorgeous in these." Olivia continued to cry quietly. "I'm not sure what's up with her tonight. I hope she'll go down all right. It's your night off, isn't it? You two got any plans?"

Mick chuckled when Ceri sighed then raised his eyebrows. "Mick has threatened to pin me down and make me watch *Buffy the Vampire Slayer*."

Olivia's cries increased and she wriggled in her mother's arms.

"Here," Ceri said. "Pass her over to me. My brother says I have a way with grizzling babies because I was one myself."

Sally didn't hesitate. "Knock yourself out. Perhaps she's hungry. I've got a bottle made up I expressed earlier."

"Give it here. I'll sit in the front room with her and see how we get on."

Minutes later, Mick listened as Ceri sang to the baby. He didn't know if it was working on Olivia, but he could feel his own eyes closing. Shaking himself out of eavesdropping, Mick turned to Sally. "I'll sort out the salad to go with the pasta. Is Phil working tonight?"

"Yes, his paternity leave is over, so it's just me and her." She paused. "Thank God for Ceri. She hasn't started crying again. He certainly has a way with her, doesn't he? D'you think you two will have children after you're married?"

"I don't know. I haven't considered it before, but I think Ceri wants to. We haven't been together long, and it's not as if we're rushing into marriage. We haven't even lived together yet. There's Ceri's application and my mum to consider. Lots of things are up in the air."

"Will you go to Leeds with him if he gets in? I'll miss you now I've only just found you again, but I'll understand."

The phone rang and Olivia, disturbed by the noise, started to cry again. "I'll get it," Sally said. In the kitchen, Mick sorted the salad, adding a few more colorful types of vegetables to make it less green.

"Mick." Sally appeared at the door and handed him the phone. "It's the hospice. Your mum has taken a turn for the worse and has asked to see you. You'd better go."

Flustered, Mick put down the knife. "Yes, okay, tell them I'll be there as soon as I can."

Ceri appeared at the door with Olivia. "I'll take you," he said. "I'll get the stuff for the bike. Surely, it's good she wants to see you, isn't it?"

Mick shook his head. "In some ways, but it probably means she thinks she's about to die. She might not want to make up with me even now, but regardless, I've got to see her this last time."

At the hospice, the helper who'd pushed her wheelchair that day took him to his mother's room. "My name is Concita. I've been helping with caring for Mrs. Flanagan for a while. She doesn't trust many people. You need to understand she's on a lot of medication and may not be conscious for long and it's difficult to tell what she's saying sometimes. Every person is different when they think their time is near, but she's been saying she's ready, and that usually means people won't fight anymore. Her breathing is shallow, and she's on oxygen, but she doesn't like the mask. She may not be able to talk, but she can hear you."

"You go in with her," Ceri said. "I'll wait outside unless you need me." He kissed him gently.

Mick squeezed Ceri's hand then entered the room behind Concita where his mother lay close to death. He took in her surroundings. The room was strangely bright. Shouldn't death beds be in dark rooms, with the curtains closed and everyone dressed in dark colors, as the dying person breathed their last? It always seemed to be that way in films. Concita gestured him to sit in the chair next to the bed. His mother had an oxygen mask over her face. With shaking hands, she signaled Concita to remove it. Mick wasn't sure what he'd expected. He didn't know how they did things in hospices. His only other real experience of death had been Alfie's, and he hadn't had even had time to process Alfie was dead because it had all happened so quickly.

"Mum, I came as you asked. I'm glad you did. I wanted to tell you I love you, and I forgive you. Nothing else matters now."

His mother tried to speak, but her voice rasped.

"It's all right, Mum, you don't need to say anything. I'll be here as long as you need me."

She glanced at the glass on the table.

"D'you want this?" Mick held the straw between her lips as she took a little sip. Then he took her hand. It felt cold, and the skin was dry and papery. *In for a penny, in for a pound.* He'd told her the important things, so he may as well tell her the rest.

"I'm not sure if you want to hear this, Mum, but I'm getting married. We haven't decided when yet. I know you don't approve of me and how I live my life, and I understand more about why now. I know you wanted a girl, and you tried to pretend I was one for as long as you could, but, Mum, I need you to understand that you didn't make me gay. I was born this way. It's nothing to do with you. And I'm happy. I've got Ceri, and I met Sally again. Yes, I know you didn't like her, but she's married now and has a little girl — Olivia. She doesn't have much hair yet, but she's a beautiful baby. Ceri is so good with her, and she always goes to sleep in his arms. We've even talked about having children."

"Does he love you?" The question came out in a quiet whisper and took Mick by surprise.

"Yes, he tells me he does and shows me in lots of different ways. I wasn't in a good place when I met him, but he's been so wonderful. He's here if you want to meet him."

She pulled her hand out from underneath his. "Hot."

"D'you want me to call Concita?" he asked. She shook her head slowly and closed her eyes. For a while, he wasn't sure what to do. He could still hear her breathing. Should he put the mask back over her face? Instead, he sat and waited for a while. After twenty minutes, Ceri put his head around the door. Mick gestured for him to come in.

"I think she's asleep," he explained. "Concita said she was in and out of consciousness. She asked if you loved me."

"I hope you told her more than anything else in the whole world." He kissed Mick on the top of his head then sat in the chair next to his.

"Something similar. I don't think she's got long, Ceri. I think she's given up now. At least she's letting me stay. I'd hate to think of her dying all by herself. She's so young, but she looks so tired."

Mick sat holding Ceri's hand, watching over his mother for the next few hours while staff came in and out making checks. When she became disturbed and talked nonsense to herself, they gave her more morphine.

"D'you think she'll talk again?" Mick asked the nurse.

"There's no way to know. We've checked her vitals, and everything is slowing down. The chances are she won't wake up again. Talk to her. She still may be able to hear your voice."

While Ceri stepped out to make some phone calls, Mick told his mother about his stories and how he hoped to get them published. He told her tales of Carlos and the Space Buccaneers, leaving out anything he thought she might not like. He also talked about his childhood and how she'd looked after him and kept him safe. Later, Ceri returned, and he leaned his head on Ceri's shoulder. Outside, the light faded, and Concita came in to close the curtains. The room felt even more enclosed now. Sometimes his mother moved around and mumbled, but he was sure she now had no idea they were there. Then there was silence. Both he and Ceri had been close to dozing off themselves. Mick noticed the difference first and jumped up.

"I think she's stopped breathing, Ceri. Will you get someone?" Ceri hurried out of the door. Mick wetted the back of his hand and put it next to her lips. There was nothing, and her chest wasn't moving either. He kissed her cheek and sat back down. Seconds later, Ceri came back in, accompanied by the nurse.

She checked for a pulse and shook her head. "She's gone," she said. "It was good you were here." She tidied up the bed then left them in the room. Ceri took Mick into his arms and let him weep. After a few minutes, someone new came in.

"Mr. Flanagan," she said, offering her hand. "I'm sorry for your loss. My name is Dr. Gemma Brownley. I've been looking after your mother whilst she's been here. I need to make a few checks and sort out the information for the death certificate. We won't need to do a post-mortem because she's been receiving treatment."

Mick nodded. "I've no idea what she wanted. I don't even know if she'd made any arrangements for her funeral or if she's written a will. I know my grandmother was buried, so I guess she'd want to be buried with her. I don't even know who to ask."

"We'll probably have some information here. People often discuss their wishes." As she went through the formalities, the manager came in. They followed her to the main office and drank the proffered tea, obviously made sweet for the purpose. Mick explained how he had no idea about the practicalities.

"We have the name of the funeral director. Someone will collect your mother's body and visit you. She left information about what she wanted. I think it's straightforward, as she wasn't expecting anyone to be there. This is the contact number. Give them a ring in the morning. I would suggest you go home now and get some rest. I know the circumstances weren't easy for you, but at least you could be here at the end."

* * * *

Around midnight, Ceri wheeled the bike into the garage. They found Sally feeding Olivia in the kitchen. She looked up when they came in.

"She died about an hour ago," Mick said. "She simply faded away."

Sally reached out a hand and touched his arm. "It's better this way. Get some sleep, the pair of you. You both look shattered."

Mick stood and stumbled up the stairs to his bedroom. Unable to focus, he let Ceri doing most of the work undressing him. Finally, he snuggled into Ceri's arms in the narrow bed, needing the warmth and safety of his body next to him, before he fell asleep and escaped his whirling mind.

Chapter Seventeen

In the end, the funeral proved simple. His mother had planned everything with the funeral directors. She'd never been one for organized religion, so he wasn't surprised to find out that she'd arranged for a humanist celebrant. However, he was surprised the woman had regularly visited his mother in the hospice. At least it meant someone who knew her would be taking the service. It took place in the funeral home in a special room set aside for the purpose. Mick wasn't sure what to expect. His mother hadn't booked any cars, just a hearse. He supposed she didn't expect anyone to need them. Instead, Sally and Phil took them. Ceri took Mick's hand as they entered the building and gave it a squeeze.

"It'll be all right," he said.

Mick just nodded. He had no words.

Inside, a handful of people from the hospice greeted them. He thanked everyone for coming. He also noticed their neighbor, Mr. Brown, sitting to one side. The service was brief and to the point. He almost smiled when he saw that the cardboard coffin. It was typical of his mother to choose such a receptacle. As he stood at the internment later, he wasn't sure how he felt. He threw the soil into the grave then leaned his head against Ceri's shoulder. Only Sally and Phil came with them to the burial. Sally patted his arm then walked off with Phil, leaving just Ceri and himself standing there. The day was glorious. It was one of those days when the sun shone but it wasn't too hot. Dappled light moved across the grass as the branches of the trees swayed in the breeze. It struck him that it was the perfect day for a walk in the countryside or a stroll along a beach.

"How long d'you think it would take for us to get to the seaside?" he asked Ceri. "We could go on your bike and stay somewhere." He needed to be anywhere but there.

"Umm, okay. Neither of us are working until tomorrow night and it shouldn't take us long to get to the seaside. Where do you fancy going?" Ceri asked. "You said you wanted to go back to Cardiff. We could get to the Welsh coast in just over an hour."

Childhood memories of his mother had kept Mick awake over the last week. He'd found one he remembered fondly. "There is somewhere I'd like to visit. Mum and I didn't go on holiday, but we did go to Burnham-on-Sea for a day trip. I don't know why we went there in particular, but I remember a huge beach, eating ice cream and building sandcastles with my mum. She bought me a red bucket and spade. I was even allowed to paddle in the water. People rode on carts pulled along the beach by parachutes. Could we go there, do you think? There are lots of bed and breakfast places, so I expect we could find somewhere for tonight."

Ceri wrapped his arms around Mick and hugged him. "You know me. I can always be persuaded to eat ice cream. Sounds like a plan. Let's do it."

Within a couple of hours, they found themselves on the expansive beach eating fish and chips out of newspaper. The sands stretched for miles and the sea was some distance away.

"These are good," Ceri said. "Remember the last time we sat on a beach at Barry Island eating out of paper? That seems so long ago now. I'll fetch us ice creams when we've finished these, then we can have a walk."

People were scattered here and there, some couples like themselves strolling on the sand and some with some families making sandcastles. Mick wanted to take Ceri's hand, but he still worried it was too public for such a display and he wanted to enjoy the day, not have someone make a comment or glower at them. He envied the couples he saw who strolled hand in hand or arm in arm without fear and wondered if things would ever change. They didn't speak. Mick thought about his mother and Ceri left him to those thoughts — there if Mick needed him.

Was it all bad? He believed his mum had loved him, but with that love came control — a control he'd thought was so normal that when Alfie treated him in the same way, he didn't question it. He'd become an anxious child without knowing any difference. The thought of disagreeing with someone seemed impossible. He glanced at Ceri. This man had offered him everything, but asked rather than demanded. He'd shown Mick how life could be different. He hoped Ceri would hear from Leeds about his application soon.

In the past, he'd have been terrified of change but now he found himself looking forward to visiting new places and buying a house where he could display his belongings. He'd submitted his story but was still waiting to hear from the publisher. Apparently, these things took time because they received so many manuscripts and selected less than ten percent. Ceri and Sally had read more of his stories and loved them, saying they had an innocent charm despite the content.

"If you get into Leeds, I want to come with you," Mick said, finally articulating his thoughts.

Ceri stopped and hugged him not caring who saw. "Good, I want you to come. We could get somewhere to live together, and you could write. I didn't want to push you into anything, and you've only just met Sally again, but—"

"I don't want a long-distance relationship," Mick said. "So, it's agreed. Even if you don't get into Leeds, wherever you go, I'm coming with you. I'm not losing you. I love you and I want to spend the rest of my life with you. I can afford to buy us somewhere..." Ceri put up his hands in protest.

"No, don't worry," Mick continued. "We can work out how to share bills and things, and you can be near your sister. I'm sure you'll get in. Your application was brilliant. They'd be stupid not to have you. Why don't we sit over there? It feels like we've walked for miles."

They sat for a while and watched the sun dip towards the horizon.

"We'd better find somewhere to stay," Ceri said. "I noticed some places near where we left the bike." He shivered. "It's getting cooler now. If we hurry, we can book in somewhere and go for dinner."

There found several small hotels with vacancy signs, but Mick pointed out one with a rainbow in the window. The owners turned out to be a couple called Steve and Tony, who welcomed them in. They had one double available and recommended a local restaurant to have an evening meal. The room was clean and interestingly decorated.

"Your dark red hair fits right in with the décor," Mick said, when they entered.

It had a surprisingly roomy ensuite, and they took advantage of the large shower enclosure then hurried to the restaurant, which proved to be as lovely as their hosts had suggested.

"I'm not sure I can make it back to the hotel," Ceri said. "I'm so stuffed full of pasta and tiramisu."

As often happened at this time of year, a warm day had turned into a cooler night as they strolled.

"Are you all right?" Ceri asked. "You didn't say much during dinner."

"Sorry. I didn't mean to. While we were on the beach this afternoon, I noticed a young lad building sandcastles with his mother. Sometimes, when I think about the past, it all seems so unreal, like it wasn't me. I feel like I'm seeing my life play out like a film in my head. Maybe I'm trying to distance myself from it—I don't know. More for me to discuss with the counselor, I guess." He shivered. "And we've so much future to look forward to now. Mum's gone and at least I was there at the end, but now it's time to move on."

"You were there, and in the end, you did your best for her," Ceri said. "I haven't mentioned it with everything going on, but my parents want you to come to Monmouth and stay as soon as so they can meet you. I wasn't sure if you were ready yet. They're pretty laid-back for teachers and it's coming up to Whitsun half-term soon."

Mick spotted the need in Ceri's voice and expression. "I'd love to meet them. I'm looking forward to meeting all your family, especially Megan. You've told me so much about them." *More planning. More future.*

Back at the guesthouse, they made love quietly, taking care of each other's needs with Mick spooned behind Ceri, bringing him to orgasm, coming himself, while pressing skin against skin and his lips to Ceri's neck and shoulders. It proved to be a good end to a sad day, and both men were glad they had decided to have the day to themselves in this place which meant something happy to Mick. They both slept soundly wrapped in each other's arms oblivious to anyone else in the world.

Breakfast was served until nine in the morning. All but one of the tables were occupied when they walked into the room rather sheepishly, having enjoyed the shower once more, just before service was over.

"Tea or coffee, gentlemen?"

"Tea, please for two," Mick said.

"Did you sleep well?"

"We did," Mick said, feeling his face redden.

"Probably all the fresh air we got yesterday," Ceri added, grinning from ear to ear.

Tony brought them a pot of tea and took their orders. Mick still found it difficult not to have his cereal on a weekday, but Ceri insisted that they try the full English breakfast he could see the other guests tucking into. Mick had to admit the bacon smelt wonderful.

"All local produce," Tony assured them. "And Steve is a great cook."

A man leaned over from the adjacent table. "Have it all," he said. "These sausages are to die for, and the scrambled eggs are so fluffy they could float away like a cloud. I'll need to run a marathon to work off this many calories, but it's so worth it." The man stared directly at Ceri and added, "Mind you, you must work out all the time with your body shape."

Mick resisted the temptation to growl but sat up in his seat. Ceri put his hand on Mick's thigh before replying.

"Oh, I'm one of those lucky buggers who can eat anything they want and not put on a pound."

Tony arrived and placed the fully loaded plates on the table. Mick shoved a forkful of food into his mouth and chewed slowly.

When he'd finished, Ceri rubbed his stomach. "That was truly amazing. I don't think I could eat another mouthful."

As he spoke, Tony brought toast and jam and placed it on the table. "Steve makes the bread and jam himself. He'd churn the butter if he had the time. Enjoy."

Ceri gazed at the toast for all of two seconds then pounced, spreading the bread with liberal quantities of butter and jam. Mick did the same. He groaned, tasting the sweetness of the strawberries.

"It's no good I've decided to leave you for Steve—this food is so good," Mick said. "Or I'll have to make my own bread. I could get a bread maker. I've never really cooked gourmet food, but I guess I could learn, take a course while you're at classes."

"You can do anything you want," Ceri said. "Everything is your decision. The world is your lobster!"

Mick looked puzzled for a moment, sure the saying was oyster, not lobster. "No, it's *our* decision. We talk about everything, all right? People have always decided for me, so I didn't know how to do anything for myself. Now, I want to talk about things. I'll still need help. Just coming here for the day is out of the ordinary for me."

Mick was sure Ceri had noticed but said nothing about how he'd made sure everything was the same in the room now as when they'd arrived, even down to the position of the glass in the bathroom. Mick had turned down using the shampoo sachet and felt uncomfortable when Ceri had taken the shower gel they'd used from the basket. It was still hard for him to leave any trace of his existence anywhere. Would it be different when they had their own home, somewhere that would belong to them? For the first time, Mick would have a space that he could make his own, somewhere he could write. He could choose colors and patterns, but one thing he knew for certain was that there would be no white.

* * * *

Back in Cheltenham, for the next couple of weeks, they waited — waited to hear from the university and waited to hear from the publisher. Neither of them had any control over *those* decisions.

Mick arrived back at Sally's after work on the Thursday morning and went to bed as usual. Ceri was due there in the afternoon so they could babysit Olivia.

Sally wanted to do the weekly shop, and they'd volunteered.

"Ceri's here," Sally called to the kitchen as she left. Mick rocked Olivia in her seat while she gurgled.

"Your Uncle Ceri is here," he said. He heard another voice as Ceri said, "Thank you," and the front door shut.

Ceri entered the kitchen clutching several letters, kissed Mick on the top of his head and sat next to him at the table. He put the three letters in front of him, two addressed to Mick and one to Ceri. Mick had arranged for all his post to be forwarded to Sally's now that the flat had sold. Ceri must have brought the other one.

Mick glanced at Ceri, unsure what to do first. He picked one up. "This one is from the publisher," he said. "Is yours from the university?"

"Yes," Ceri nodded. "I asked them to send a letter as the internet is often unpredictable at my house. Will you open it for me? I can't face doing it."

"I'll do you a swop. I'll open yours if you open mine."

"What about this one?" Ceri asked. "It's from a solicitor."

"It's probably something about the flat. I've filled in so many forms for the sale. They said they'd be sending a satisfaction form for me to fill in."

Mick picked up his mug and swallowed some tea to fortify himself. He had no real expectation that the publisher would like his stories. "Okay, let's open them and take out the letters." He ran his finger along the inside of the top of the envelope and pulled out the folded letter. Ceri did the same.

"Well?" Ceri asked. "What does it say? Did I get a place?" He crossed his fingers as Mick unfolded the A4 piece of paper. Mick scanned it for a moment then smiled. "You got in. They've offered you a place for the next academic year. You did it. We're off to Leeds." Mick reached across and hugged Ceri.

"Let me see," Ceri said. "I'm not sure I can take it in." Mick passed him the letter.

"It's all there in black and white. I told you they'd be stupid not to have you. Megan will be thrilled. At least we've got a few months to get things organized and find somewhere to live." He let Ceri absorb the information before turning his attention to the other letter.

"Okay, my turn. Tell me the worst." Mick waited, tapping his fingers on the table, while Ceri carefully read the letter. He hadn't yet set anything up online for himself. "They've rejected it, haven't they? It's all right. I was expecting it. They're only stupid stories."

Ceri put a finger to his lips. "They haven't rejected it," he mumbled.

"What? They want to publish?" Mick wanted to get up and dance around the room.

"Hang on. You need to read this. There's lots of stuff here about how much they like the stories, but I think they want you to change the target audience. It looks like they want you to write for teenagers rather than adults. Could you do that?"

Mick couldn't help feeling a little deflated. "Let me see," he said. He took the letter and read it. He was relieved to read they didn't want to change the characters, as there was no way that Carlos and his captain would not be together in his stories. *Can I do what they want? I can try.*

They wanted some re-writes as soon as possible and had said they were very excited about the work. The letter named an editor for him to contact who worked in this market. He would have to change some aspects, but the basic stories and characters could stay the same. Suddenly, he had visions of becoming the new name in youth-orientated literature. He tried to picture Carlos on the screen fighting his way across the cosmos.

"You're already planning it, aren't you?" Ceri said. "This is so amazing. My boyfriend, the famous writer."

"Let's not get ahead of ourselves," Mick said. "They may not like the changes. I might have to submit to another publisher. Some authors have to submit to loads of publishers before one takes them."

Ceri picked up the remaining envelope. "Here, you'd better open this before we celebrate. D'you hear that, Olivia? Your Uncle Mick is going to become a famous author."

Mick opened the other letter. "Oh my God!" He put it down then picked it up again.

"What is it?" Ceri asked, with a worried expression.

"It's to do with Mum. I didn't even think... I thought she'd have left everything to some charity, but this says she left everything to me. Bloody hell, Ceri, she left me the house, and it seems there's money too. I've got to sign some documents then it's all mine. I don't believe it. Despite everything, she left it to me. Perhaps she forgave me after all." Tears rolled down his cheeks. "We missed so much, Ceri, and as soon as I found her again, cancer took her away. I wish she was here to know others will get to read my stories. I wish she could have been proud of me."

Ceri took his hand. "I'm proud of you, and I love you so much. Bloody hell." He glanced toward the baby. "Sorry."

"I don't think she'll be up to learning new words yet," Mick said, wiping his eyes.

"But don't you see? This means you can just spend your time writing. You've got enough stories for so many books. I hope they put pictures in. Who d'you think should play Carlos and the captain in the film? Tell you what, though, you'll have to take out the scene when they celebrate after grabbing the treasure from the Many-Spotted Bangaloos. You know, the one in the zero-gravity room, when Carlos finds out what happens if you don't swallow."

Mick grinned. "Oh yeah, that could be tricky, but like everything else in our future, it'll be such fun."

Epilogue

Eighteen months later

"Are we mad?" Mick asked Sally as he pulled on the last part of his outfit. "We had to toss a coin to see which of us got to be Captain Jack and which the Doctor. I know I don't look like him but who wouldn't want to get married in a greatcoat?"

Sally fussed around him, already dressed as River Song, while Olivia, dressed in her Thirteenth Doctor costume, sat on the floor mumbling to herself. "It's your wedding and this is what you want – what brought you together. I've checked on the room this morning and the venue is beautiful. And who wouldn't want to get married in a museum where they filmed *Doctor Who*?"

"Some people might think it's a waste of money."

"And some people should keep their views to themselves. You and Ceri deserve the best. Anyway, your book is selling like hot cakes since its release. Your agent is earning every penny of her fee to get you onto radio and television. Social media is full of comments about diversity and representation. Sometimes, I pinch myself when I hear you over the airwaves."

She straightened his tie. "There you are. Except for the hair and beard, Captain Jack Harkness personified." She scooped Olivia from the floor. "We'd better get a move on or we'll be late. Phil's bringing the car around. Wait until you see his outfit."

Mick waited with Sally and Olivia at the entrance to their hotel. Fortunately, though cold, this December day in Cardiff turned out to be sunny, which was just as well when Mick spotted a car entering the driveway of the hotel.

"Oh. My. God. Where did you even?"

"Surprise," Sally said. "It's our present to you for the day. We found it online, and the owner hires it out for weddings. With Phil being a trained police driver, he let him drive."

Mick stared at the perfect replica of the Third Doctor's car, a canary yellow Roadster named Bessie. He hurried down the steps with his greatcoat billowing around him.

"She's beautiful," he said, running his hand down the bonnet. "And exactly like the original." He hugged Sally. "Thank you. I can't believe you did this for us. It's even got a child seat in the front for Olivia."

"Are we ready then?" Phil said. He wore the uniform of Brigadier Lethbridge-Stewart, a much-loved character from *Old Who*.

Mick and Sally sat in the back. On the short journey to the museum, people waved at them as they passed, and they waved back. Mick felt his excitement growing. They'd agreed that Ceri would wait for Mick inside the venue, a specially chosen room within the museum, with his family, some friends from Leeds, and others from the building where Mick had worked in Cheltenham. He wished Tommy could have been there, but he and Ceri intended to visit him on their way back to help him celebrate reaching one hundred years old as well as laying flowers on Mick's mother's grave.

They pulled up at the steps in front of the National Museum of Wales. "I'll see you inside," Phil said. "I have a secure place to leave the car so you and Ceri can have a quick drive around after the service to wave to a few more people. I know Ceri wouldn't want to miss riding in her, and we can get Bessie in the photographs before we eat."

Mick slipped his arm through Sally's as they climbed the steps at the front of the museum and made their way through the building. Ifan, Ceri's brother, greeted at the entrance to the venue, dressed as the Ninth Doctor, along with his two boys. Mick laughed out loud.

"They insisted," Ifan said. "They wanted to be Daleks following you up the aisle shouting *exterminate*, if that's all right with you. Ceri thought you'd like it."

"I do." Mick knelt in front of the boys. "You look awesome," he said. "And so do you, Ifan. Ceri would have dressed as the Ninth Doctor, but he didn't want to cut his hair so short. Thank you for indulging us."

Ifan grinned. All the siblings resembled one another and had the same blue eyes. "Wait until you see the others," Ifan continued. "Everyone looks amazing. Dylan wanted to come as a Slitheen, but he couldn't find a costume, so he's dressed as the newest Master."

Mick turned back to the boys. "Thank you both for joining in. I would love it if you followed me and Sally.

Maybe you could take a hand each for Olivia and she could walk with you."

"You can do that?" Ifan said. "It's a very important job." They both nodded earnestly.

The boys stood with Olivia in front of Mick and Sally to make sure everything was all right. Ifan held the door open for them and they stepped inside. Mick gazed around the room taking everything in. Various paintings from the museum had been borrowed to decorate the walls, including a Van Gogh, though sadly not *Sunflowers* or *Starry Night*. Strings of *Doctor Who* themed flags with images of aliens and characters hung across the room. He glanced down the aisle where Ceri stood in his Tenth Doctor costume. Mick's heart skipped a beat. They were doing this. They were getting married with these witnesses all dressed in various costumes. Even Ceri's parents had agreed to dress up as the original Master and Romana.

The music began with Jack's theme, *The Doctor and Me*. Mick walked slowly to the front with shaking knees until he stood side by side with Ceri in front of the registrar.

"You look wonderful," Ceri said. "I love a man in a swishy coat."

"You too," Mick said. "I see you wore the blue suit, not brown. It brings out the color of your eyes, but maybe we should take off the coats now." Ceri nodded, and they handed them over to Dylan, Ceri's other brother, who sat with his wife and children. Behind Ceri stood Megan, his twin sister, dressed as the Sixth Doctor complete with a multi-colored jacket and curly wig. She grinned at him. No doubt Sophie would be somewhere in the congregation. Only direct family had been asked to dress up, but Sophie had joined in as well and had come as a much taller version of Sarah Jane Smith, complete with dark wig and red and white striped dungarees. With everyone else seated, Mick took Ceri's hand, and they faced forward.

The ceremony didn't take long. They made their vows and exchanged rings and suddenly it was all over. *I'm married. I'm really married to this wonderful man. Two years ago, I had nothing and now I have all this.*

"You may kiss the Doctor," the registrar said.

"Mick?" Ceri's voice brought him out of his thoughts.

"Sorry, it's just I can't believe how lucky I am."

Ceri wrapped his arms around Mick, pulling him close. "We're both lucky. Now kiss me while everyone is looking."

Mick did as Ceri instructed. The kiss was brief but beautiful. The congregation clapped, whooped and whistled, and Mick never wanted it to end. Olivia, however, had other ideas. She escaped the control of the boys and pulled at Mick's trousers.

"Unca Mick, Unca Mick. Carry me." He tore away from Ceri and picked her up. Sally moved forward to rescue him.

"Car," Olivia said. Mick grinned.

"I've a surprise for you," Mick said, glancing at Phil who nodded and rushed off outside.

"I hate to interrupt, but you need to sign the register before anything else." The registrar led them to a table to sign and have more photographs taken. Ceri stood to announce what would happen next.

"We're having photographs taken outside while they set up for the meal and speeches in here. So, if you'd follow us out without rushing…"

Mick and Ceri led the way down the aisle and to the entrance. The canary Roadster waited for them outside.

"It's Bessie," Ceri said, dragging Mick down the steps. "How?"

"Phil sorted it. He drove us here. He says he'll give us a runaround before he has to return it. But first more photographs." They turned to see their guests behind them. Flower petals rained down as the photographer clicked his camera. After what seemed like three thousand different poses, Ceri joined Mick in the back of the car. Phil drove them around a few streets past the castle and down to the university buildings.

"I feel like the Queen," Ceri said, as he waved again. "It's not exactly a golden coach but..."

"No, it's much better," Mick said. "I suppose we have to go back and can't just sneak back to the hotel for a couple of hours before tonight's buffet and disco."

"Don't even think about it," Phil warned. "Damn, this mustache keeps falling off."

"Keep your hands on the wheel," Mick called.

The trip was too short. By the time they returned, everyone was back inside. Mick took Ceri's hand, and they strolled up the steps, not caring who stared. "This is our day," he whispered. "I can't remember feeling this happy in my life."

Ceri halted Mick outside the door. "I love you so much, Mick Flanagan, and everyone in there loves you too. Remind me to hug Ruby. Without her, I wouldn't have come to your office that day." He maneuvered Mick back against the wall, pressed his body close and kissed Mick hard. Mick responded, wrapping his arms around Ceri, feeling his erection, knowing he was half hard too. The door opened, and they jumped apart.

"I might have bloody guessed," Megan said. "Can't you wait until tonight? Everyone is starving and we're waiting for you and the speeches before we get stuck in." She grabbed their hands and led them into the room to more cheers and whistles and escorted them to the top table. Mick held the chair back for Ceri then sat next to him.

Over the next couple of hours, speeches were made, food was eaten, stories were told and several people downed rather too much champagne. Ceri leaned into Mick.

"I think I'm gonna need a little lie down." He picked up his glass. "These buddles, I mean bubbles, keep going up my nose."

"And down your throat," Ceri's mother said.

"Always was a lightweight," his father added.

Around the edge of the room, the staff hovered. "I think it's time we left," Mick said. He stood and tapped the glass.

"Just to say to everyone, we're back to the hotel now. The buffet will be in the main room at seven this evening with the disco starting about eight. I believe there will be karaoke for the brave as well. My husband and I would like to thank you for your cards and gifts, the donations to our chosen charities and for sharing this day with us. Dress is more casual this evening, so come as you please. Lastly, thank you to the staff for helping us have this lovely day in this special place. And that's part one complete."

* * * *

"It's a gorgeous room," Ceri said, spinning around so much he toppled over onto the bed. "Why don't you come over here and join me? I'm sure we can find something to occupy us for the next couple of hours."

"Clothed or unclothed?" Mick asked. It still took him unawares, being so bold.

Ceri leaned on one side, holding himself up on his elbow, a beaming smile on his face and a mischievous look in his eyes. "Strip for me," he said, slowly licking his lips.

The action went straight to Mick's cock.

"As you wish, Doctor. I will defabricate immediately." Mick slipped off his shoes and socks, then edged the red braces languorously over each shoulder, leaving them hanging from his trousers. Undoing each button of his blue shirt revealed more of his hairy chest. In the past, being so hirsute had embarrassed him, but Ceri loved winding his fingers in the curls. Mick turned, slipped the shirt from each arm and down his back while giving his arse a wiggle.

"Oh, Captain Jack. You are such a tease. Why don't you show me that gorgeous bottom of yours?"

Mick undid his belt then the buttons and slowly lowered his trousers inch by inch. Ceri moaned, sending more blood rushing to Mick's now prominent erection. He stepped out then turned, now totally naked, to find Ceri rubbing his crotch.

"Couldn't wait, huh?" he said.

"Looks like I'm not the only one. Give me a moment." And a moment was all Ceri needed to remove his clothes except for the tie hanging around his neck. He patted the bed. "Lie down. I intend to give you the ride of your life."

Mick leaped on the bed. Ceri immediately straddled him, leaned over, kissed him and tweaked Mick's nipple.

"Ouch!"

"Aww, did I pinch a bit hard? Here, let me soothe it." Ceri moved back so their cocks rubbed together, then moved to and fro, kissing and licking Mick's nipple as he did.

"Need to be inside you," Mick said.

"And you shall be, my husband. Wow, I love saying that."

"You've no idea how much I love hearing it."

Ceri reached under the pillow and pulled out the lube he'd secreted there earlier. They no longer used condoms. The first time they'd fucked without, Mick had been overwhelmed that Ceri would afford him that level of trust. Now, he lay back, watching Ceri prep himself as he liked to do when they made love in this position. Mick stroked himself, keeping himself hard and ready, not that seeing Ceri with three fingers in his arse didn't keep him as hard as iron.

Ceri withdrew, spread more lube on Mick's cock, then positioned his body so he slipped down in one go until Mick was fully enclosed.

"I love you so much," he said, bending over to kiss Mick. "Now, fuck me, husband, and make me come all over you."

Mick thrust up, meeting Ceri's downward movements. "God, I love this. It feels different now we're married."

"Oh yeah, just there, that's the spot." Ceri groaned. He took hold of his cock and stroked himself. "Nearly there. Can you come with me?"

Mick increased his pace. Tingles ran down his spine into his balls. "Close," he said. Ceri lifted one hand and squeezed a nipple. Mick lurched.

"That's it. Oh, God." With one final thrust, his climax tore out of him. Ceri threw his head back and came, sending ropes of white liquid over Mick's stomach.

"Yes, oh yes. I can feel you filling me." Ceri slumped over, letting Mick's cock slip out, and lay on Mick's chest breathing heavily before finally rolling over.

"We'll need a shower," Ceri said, cuddling into Mick's side. Mick's eyes felt heavy. He yawned.

"Hmm, yeah. In a minute," he said. "Just have a lie-down."

* * * *

"What the..." The banging noise continued. Ceri groaned. Mick shook him. "Ceri, we fell asleep. Ugh, I'm all crusty."

"Mick, Ceri, where are you? We're waiting for you."

Sally. He hurried off the bed, grabbed a robe, covered himself and opened the door enough to see his friend. "Sorry, we were tired. Give us fifteen and we'll be with you."

Sally grinned. "Hmm, I bet. Anyway, get your arses literally into gear. But before you do, I might suggest a quick shower. Nothing like a session of afternoon delight to pass the time." She turned and strolled down the corridor, whistling.

Fifteen minutes later, washed and dressed as promised, Mick took Ceri's hand. "You look so handsome," he said. "Though I'm still getting used to you having brown hair."

"I know, back to my original color. I couldn't be the Tenth Doctor with blue hair, not even TARDIS blue. Are we ready?"

Mick reached up and cupped Ceri's face. They touched lips briefly. "Thank you for everything."

Ceri grinned. "Right back at you." He pushed open the door into the function room and every face turned toward them. In the past Mick would have turned tail and run, but now, with his hand firmly in Ceri's hand, he walked to the front of the room.

"Thank goodness," Megan said. "I'm starving and this buffet smells wonderful."

Mick picked up a glass and hit it lightly with a spoon to get people's attention. "Hello, everyone. I see we've been joined by a few others who couldn't make this afternoon. The buffet is open and the dancing will start at eight, so tuck in."

The people moved as one.

"Do weddings make people especially hungry?" he asked Ceri.

"From what I've seen, it's the same with funerals and christenings. All I'm looking forward to is our first dance together."

"I'm so glad we took those lessons," Mick said.

"We'd better mingle with our guests first, though."

Mick spent some time with Wilf and Ruby as well as his agent and some other authors he'd met over the last few months, filling in the time until the first dance. The DJ introduced himself and called for Mick and Ceri to come to the floor.

"Come on," Ceri said.

The room darkened except for a shiny spinning globe on the ceiling which sent out small sparkles of light over the wooden floor. They faced each other. Ceri kissed the wedding ring nestled on Mick's finger.

"I know we're not in costume anymore, but you, Mick Flanagan, are my perfect companion. Thank you for making me the happiest man in the world."

"And you, Ceri Llewellyn, are mine. Who would have believed being a *Doctor Who* fan would have brought me all this?" He gazed around the room at all the smiling faces. "And now I want you to dance with me."

As the music started, Mick thought his heart might burst with happiness. He'd spent so much of his life hiding in the shadows, on the edge of existence. Then, with tears of joy in his eyes and holding on to Ceri's hand, he pulled his perfect companion into his arms and they danced.

Want to see more from this author?
Here's a taster for you to enjoy!

Two for the Road
Alexa Milne

Excerpt

Riley tapped his fingers on the wheel of his BMW, glanced first at his watch then up the steps to the door.

"Where the hell is he?" Should he get out and knock on the door? *Why did I agree to this? Giving lifts is never wise.* Riley already knew the answer. *Because his father was my best friend. Because I'm lonely. Because...*

The black-painted door flew open and a tall, gangly red-haired youth—in Riley's eyes—rushed down the steps, attempting to push one arm through a coat sleeve while holding a piece of toast in the other. He stuffed the toast in his mouth, somehow managed the coat then turned around and ran up back up the steps to collect a bag from his mother. He flung open the passenger-side door and jumped in, placing the bag on his lap.

"I'm sorry. I've no excuse. I need to take a clock into the shower. I won't do it again, I promise. Dad's already torn a strip off me."

Riley smiled. He'd never admit it to the young man at his side, but timekeeping had never been a strong point of his youth, either. He recalled his father dragging the bedding from over him, then slammed shut the memory.

"Try not to make a habit of it." He adopted his firm but fair tone, the one he used with clients making impossible demands. Glancing sideways revealed Dylan hadn't changed much. Always skinny with a head of bright red hair and now matching beard, Dylan had been a smiling toddler when Riley had moved to London and a thin brooding teenager of fifteen when he'd last met him.

"I won't," Dylan replied cheerfully to Riley's admonition. "Should we get off? It's my first day, and I need to make a good impression."

Riley turned on the engine and slipped the car out of brake into gear. He checked in all directions and pulled out into the traffic. A light drizzle began, typical weather on the north side of Pendle Hill. The village of his childhood, and his home for the last twelve months, nestled on the side of the hill famous for its witches. He negotiated his way out of the village and onto the motorway. The drizzle turned to rain pattering on the windscreen.

"Thanks for agreeing to give me a lift. I hope it's not too much of a pain, and I'll try not to be irritating."

Riley didn't reply, hoping to stop the conversation. He was used to quiet journeys accompanied only by the radio or a CD if he felt so inclined. He'd expected Dylan to pull out his mobile, stick in headphones and amuse himself. Dylan, however, didn't take the hint.

"You doing this is such a relief. I panicked when I got the job, but beggars can't be choosers these days, and I'm lucky to have one at all. Dad said he'd sort something out for me, and he did, thanks to you. You and him go way back, he told me, but you left to live in London. I remember you visiting a few years back?"

Riley had no chance to reply.

"I've only been once, you know, to London. I bet you know all the good places, theaters, restaurants, museums, clubs? I didn't plan to come back here, but I got the job in Preston, so here I am. Hopefully, I'll be able move out of home to somewhere nearer, or with a railway station when I've saved enough. I went to Durham University, but I expect you know that."

Riley did, but only because Tony had come to his father's funeral several months back. The meeting had been awkward. He'd been back six months already at that point, taking care of his father as he gradually faded away. Any guilt he'd felt about not reaching out to his oldest friend had disappeared when Tony hadn't contacted him, either. He nodded, knowing Dylan would continue.

"I loved Durham, but there weren't any jobs there. I miss my university friends, but we're determined to meet up. I bet you got up to all sorts at uni in London."

Ah, the past. Riley sighed. He'd never be able to stand this onslaught every morning, especially if it came accompanied by twenty questions. Perhaps it wouldn't be for long. He reached over and turned on the radio, hoping Dylan might get the message without him having to be rude and ask him to shut up.

"Oh, I love this one. You hardly ever hear Living in a Box on the radio." Dylan proceeded to join in, singing and dancing in his seat.

Did I ever have such energy? Riley felt every one of his forty-two years weighing him down.

Dylan nudged him. "Come on, don't let the side down. Join in. Didn't you and Dad used to play this together back in the day?"

Riley couldn't resist smiling and humming along. How long had it been since he'd played? His guitar lay gathering dust in one of the spare rooms. Dylan had a good voice.

"We did, but how do you know this song?" he asked. "You weren't even born."

"I bet you know all the Beatles' hits," Dylan replied.

"Yeah, but everyone does, don't they? My father was a fan. He saw them play at the Cavern Club in Liverpool." This fact had always surprised him. He couldn't picture his staid, conservative father in such a venue.

"And so, my dad still plays his stuff from the eighties. They say you never forget the songs you listened to in your early teens. I grew up with his stuff, and…" He leaned forward and whispered, "Don't tell Mum, but I liked it more than Dylan. She still plays his stuff all the time too."

Riley chuckled. "I remember her and your father discussing what to call you."

"And, Mum won. Still, it could be worse. At least she wasn't an Elvis fan. Can you imagine having to spend your life as Elvis Hargreaves? Do you still play guitar?"

Riley smiled at the memory. Their band hadn't been anything special but had still played at every school concert, even when he'd moved to the local grammar, due to a music teacher desperate to have acts willing to perform. "I haven't for a while, but I expect I could strum out a tune. I was never as good as your dad. He played lead. I was the silent, hardly moving bass player."

"Cool. I play sax. I took music at A level. It always surprises people I did math and music, but they go together somehow — chords, intervals, progression — all math. And I've always been good with figures. Some people think accountancy is boring, but I've always loved being able to manipulate numbers and see patterns. Music is the same, isn't it? The best songs use certain intervals between notes to hook you in and chord changes and sequences. If you study it properly, you can see how a song is constructed and pull it apart."

Riley pressed the accelerator to overtake the lorry on the inside lane. "You know, I've never thought about music in that way." There was certainly more to Dylan than met the eye. "I just like how it sounds. Do you still play sax?"

"For myself, but Mum worries about the neighbors complaining. I might look for a group to join. Not driving is a pain, though. Once I start getting paid, I'm gonna save up for my own car." He ran his hand over the dashboard. "Nothing like this beauty, though. I bet it even has heated seats. Good to know my arse will be nice and toasty in the winter."

Riley didn't want to think about Dylan's arse, or any other part of him. That part of his life was well and truly over.

"Maybe you and I should get together and play with Dad. Mum still sings, you know, and Kayleigh plays keyboard, though she didn't get beyond grade five. She hated having to practice, and I doubt she'll be home from university much. She can't stand living here."

"But you're all right with it?" Riley asked. Over twenty years ago, he'd had the same feelings.

"I guess so, and this way I get my food made and washing done. I know you're supposed to go to university, have experiences, develop a network and find someone. Well, I found lots of someones, but no one special, and even though I loved Durham, I've found I quite like being home too. Mum and Dad are great, and I have my old mates, Matt and Dan. With any luck, I'll meet new people at work. Are you planning to stay in the village? Dad wasn't sure, with all the memories. Looking after your father those last months must have been tough."

"It was." The last conversation he wanted to have was about watching his father fade away as the cancer took the man who'd always been so strong. He hadn't decided what to do about the house, but he couldn't return to his old life. Taking the partnership at his father's firm now tied him to the area and gave him a reason to get up every day. A face from his past flashed into Riley's mind. He pushed it away.

"Sorry, sometimes I open my mouth without thinking. Please tell me if I blather on. I'm not good with silence and tend to fill it with words. See, I'm doing it again, babbling on. Feel free to tell me to shut up."

"It's fine," Riley lied. Maybe if he let him, Dylan would get all his words out in one trip. "Truth is I haven't decided what to do with the house." He stared into the distance.

"Mr. Ormerod."

Riley braked harder than he intended, realizing the roundabout at the end of the motorway was coming up. They were both thrown forward. "Sorry about that. And please, call me Riley. My father was Mr. Ormerod." He pulled up at the first set of lights.

"D'you need me to stop at the town hall? It can sometimes be busy at this time of day. I have a parking space at my office just around the corner. I could drop you off there instead. With your long legs, it shouldn't take you long."

"Sounds good to me. Now, what about tonight? I'm supposed to finish at five. Shall I meet you at yours, or hang about outside? I could go to the library if it's raining, or there's a café opposite, if you're going to be late, or as it's flexitime, I can leave a bit later. Give me your phone, and I'll put my number in so you can call me."

This was the bit of the arrangement that had worried Riley as much as the noise, but after several solitary months, Tony's call out of the blue, asking if he could give his son a lift, had provided him with a lifeline, and Sue, his father's carer, had encouraged him to take the olive branch.

"Remind me when we get there. I usually try to finish around five, but it depends as some clients can't get to the office during the day. Most of what I do is paper, not people, but meetings can happen any time." He pulled up yet again.

"Bugger me, there are a lot of lights on these roads since they made all the changes and pedestrianized the shopping area," Dylan said. "And cameras everywhere. Dad hates driving in Preston."

"At least they've finished updating the roads around the station and built the new entrance," Riley agreed. "They've made a real effort to improve the place since it got city status, with lots of modern buildings, and it's such a big university town now — you should feel much more at home. Riley glanced across at Dylan again. He looked much more like Lori than Tony. "You know, it's funny. Of all the jobs I thought your father might do, I never figured he'd follow your granddad into his shop in Clitheroe. He hated being dragged there when we were young."

"I guess people change. He loves the place now he sells what he wants. And it turned out he has a nose for an antique. When Granddad had his stroke, Dad took over. He used to take me with him on trips to find new items. You never know when you'll get a bargain, he'd say. He's like a pig in muck at a house clearance. He's at the big auction place in Clitheroe today. By the way, I'm supposed to invite you round for dinner one night or Sunday lunch to say thank you."

Riley turned into the narrow lane behind the high street then into the car park, grateful not to have to reply. It had been tough and lonely, coming back home and caring for his dying father, a man he'd never been close to. He hadn't only come back for the man, but for himself, having nowhere else to go.

"We're here," he said, pulling up in front of the sign declaring Whewell and Ormerod, Solicitors. "Give me your mobile and we'll sort out the numbers." He exchanged numbers and gave Dylan back the phone.

"Ring me when you're ready," Dylan said.

Riley tucked the phone into his jacket pocket. "Good luck on your first day."

"Thanks. I'll see you later." Dylan clambered out of the car, threw his bag over his back and hurried off through the narrow back lane between the buildings. Riley sighed. Had he ever been that young? If he had, it was a lifetime ago.

"Bloody hell," he said, staring in the rear-view mirror. "You're forty-two, not ninety. Your life is not over." Willing himself to believe his own words, Riley picked up his briefcase, stepped out of the car and headed for the office with a spring in his step.

PUBLISHING

Sign up for our newsletter and find out about all our
romance book releases, eBook sales and promotions,
sneak peeks and FREE romance books!

About the Author

Originally from South Wales, Alexa has lived for over thirty years in the North West of England. Now retired, after a long career in teaching, she devotes her time to her obsessions.

Alexa began writing when her favourite character was killed in her favourite show. After producing a lot of fanfiction she ventured into original writing.

She is currently owned by a mad cat and spends her time writing about the men in her head, watching her favourite television programmes and usually crying over her favourite football team.

Alexa loves to hear from readers. You can find her contact information, website details and author profile page at https://www.pride-publishing.com

www.ingramcontent.com/pod-product-compliance
Lightning Source LLC
Chambersburg PA
CBHW020430180626
46812CB00003B/1165